DREAMS
OF
REFUGIUM

——————————— The Draconyma Cycle ———————————

THETA

–**DREAMS OF REFUGIUM** –

EPHEMERIS

OF DRAGONS AND STARSHIPS

WRATH

———————————————— *foxprints.org* —

DREAMS
OF
REFUGIUM

SASHA FOX

A Snowfox Press book

Published by Snowfox Press

First printing, December, 2017
ISBN: 978-0-9894414-2-1
Library of Congress Control Number: 2017918490

Cover art by Sasha Fox

Cover and Interior design ©2017, 2018, 2026 Snowfox Press

For Rox and Paradox

NON CANIMUS SURDIS, RESPONDENT OMNIA SILVAE

[Tʀᴀɴsᴄʀɪᴘᴛɪᴏɴ ᴇɴᴛʀʏ]
Wᴀʀɴɪɴɢ: Tᴇʀᴍɪɴᴀʟ ʀᴇǫᴜɪʀᴇs ᴍᴀɪɴᴛᴇɴᴀɴᴄᴇ
 >>> Tᴇʀᴍɪɴᴀʟ ʀᴇǫᴜɪʀᴇs ᴍᴀɪɴᴛᴇɴᴀɴᴄᴇ <<<

I haven't been able to hold down solid food for more than ten days, and I was starving before.

I'm probably going to die soon.

It's the dizziness that's the worst. Vomiting has me sore but numb, but the dizziness? Sometimes I just bite my pillow and sob. It never goes away, just gets a little less bad sometimes.

Most of my fear has passed now. This life wasn't meant for me. For anyone.

I pass out from exhaustion often now, but I don't get restful sleep. I have delirious dreams where I'm spinning and drowning, and then I wake up to vomit.

They did this. I know they did.

Percy came by a few days ago to bring me some cooked tubers, but he didn't seem well, either. I told him to keep them, but he told me I had to get my strength back.

I haven't heard anything from his flat today.

Well, I'm sure you don't want to read that stuff. I just wanted to leave a memoir.

One nobody will read, written by someone with nothing to write about.

Nothing else to do but sit here and die. At least transcribing helps me pretend to ignore the vertigo.

I grew up here. Not just here, the city, but right here in my flat. It was bad then. It's worse now. It used to be power outages, floods and fires. Food was scarce.

Now food is gone. Fires don't burn because there's not much to burn. Just trash.

My dad had a job, to pay for this flat. Now there's no jobs, but nobody to ask for rent money.

My dad, I think he was good. He always tried to scrounge enough for two. He taught me to fight, to stay alive.

He kept me alive, anyway.

When the Big Slide happened, he made sure I was ok. After everything stopped, we scrounged. But I always got the better of what he found. Even when there were no jobs, he was always doing something. He never told me what.

Pretty sure he died to a crazy or a robber. Maybe factory security, though I guess probably not. He just never came home one day in my sixth or seventh year, and that was that. So I had to learn how to scrounge on my own.

Pretty simple, though, when you're hungry.

Then the plagues started.

They did it. The factories.

I don't know why, but I know they did.

I was the son of Maraiki and some vixen he knocked up. She snuck out shortly after I was born. That's what he says, anyway.

Meh.

Just had a bad dizzy spell. I'm really tired now. This could be it.

DREAMS
OF
REFUGIUM

FIRST

"CONNECTING YOUR CALL."

The coyote scrunched over the terminal drummed his claws on the little fold-out dinner table beneath its display, canine visage locked in a nauseous grimace.

"I know you're there, Alain," he muttered to himself, amber eyes locked on the single, familiar word at the center of the screen.

CONNECTING.

Just a few more seconds, and the system would disconnect, as usual, and he could go on pretending that things were ok.

His ears trembled, perked to attention.

Please don't pick up . . .

His stomach sank as the word faded away and the field behind it resolved into the face of a brown-haired skunk in sharp evening wear, not a hair out of place.

"Hi! Who—" Alain's expression froze, and he pushed back from the terminal, sucking his lip between his teeth. "Geren."

Guilty, Geren thought grimly.

"Hi, Alain."

"Are you at work? No, too early. It said—who is Brodie?"

"Brodie, huh?" Geren showed his teeth in what he hoped to be a neutral grin, struggling to conceal the emotion in his voice. "He's our new bunkmate. Guess he left himself logged in. Whoops."

"I see." Alain visibly squirmed, but he was quickly recovering his composure. "I haven't heard from you for a while."

"Well, I've tried to call. A lot. Sent messages, came by once . . . I tried all last week to invite you to dinner for our a—anniversary, you know. Funny that you answered Brodie's call."

By the time Geren finished, Alain's expression had become opaque; the skunk lifted his nose slightly. "Oh?"

"I called because I was wondering if you wanted to get dinner tonight, after my shift." Geren plunged ahead, forcing the words to form and trying to make them sound normal, just in case there was a chance. "Doesn't have to be much. Just seeing you would be nice. "

The skunk drew back, and Geren held his breath, watching him assemble his defense mechanisms one at a time as though he were putting on a suit of armor.

"Geren . . . listen, I just can't do this anymore." Alain's voice was pitched to sound sad, but his words carried no genuine compassion. "Merrine doesn't want me seeing you. He said I had to choose, Geren . . . and I—Geren, I chose him. I told you how this was going months ago."

"You said there would always be a place for me," Geren's voice emerged thin and raspy, and he swallowed, trying to keep himself together as the blow finally landed. "Said you'd never abandon me . . ."

"I never said . . . you know, I knew you were going to do this." Alain switched to the attack, as he always did when cornered, voice rising in volume and tempo, though his eyes remained cool and impassive. "You know we're not compatible, you know we've had problems. You get awkward every time I'm affectionate with Merrine, anyway."

"Well, I mean—"

"No. Really, Geren. Answer this—why would you want to be around? Do you just want to torment us? Have you forgotten our arguments? I can't go on like that anymore. Listen, I can't see you again, not even socially. It's over."

Over.

Geren's mouth moved silently, but he couldn't find his voice or form a response; his ears had swiveled flat against his head and he couldn't lift them, no matter how he tried to summon a neutral expression.

Expected or not, the finality of that word left him shaken and eviscerated.

"I never wanted to hurt you." Alain's words, rendered tinny by the terminal's audio, softened, and he stared into the pickup with a carefully-crafted expression of pity. "I'm sorry you became so attached."

Unable to hold eye contact any longer, Geren looked away from the skunk's image, then flipped off the video pickup on his side with a tiny swipe gesture and sank back into the soft station chair.

He bounced his unkempt claws on the little table, heart racing.

"Oh Gerr . . ." Alain sighed.

Geren wiped his eyes. A thousand retorts cascaded through his mind, but he suppressed them all, closing his eyes in resignation.

It was done.

It was past time to let go.

"No . . . if that's how it is, that's how it is. I get it. Look, it's fine. I'll . . . survive."

"Listen . . ." Alain spoke more gently still, and Geren felt his heart lurch at the scrap of warmth. "It's nothing you did. Merrine and I . . . I'm sorry, but I just have more connection to him."

"But I—"

"No, Gerr. I tried—we tried, but . . . look, we had a bit of lust for a while, and maybe we almost had love . . . but with Merrine it just *works*, you know? It's amazing . . . it's natural."

"I'm glad you finally found someone who you're capable of loving." Geren spoke through his teeth, compelled by an upwelling of bitterness.

"Well I *do* love him, and I want this to be for life. What was I supposed to do, give that up and be miserable? Can't I just be happy? Can't you be happy for me?"

"You told me you'd always love me." Geren pounded his fist on the table, trying to mask the quaver in his voice by hardening his midsection to steel. "I've gotta go." To his shame, his voice broke; a flash of anger surged through him. "Thanks, though. Thanks for two wasted years. Glad I could sate your lust until you found someone from your own social class who'd bend over for you. I hope you two have fun—you—"

The terminal emitted a soft bleep as the connection was closed from the other end, and the frozen black-and-white of Alain's disapproving face faded back to the flat black and grey of the wall.

"You . . ." Geren dropped into his chair and sank forward, resting his slender muzzle between his paws, overcome by a bitter melange of anger and despair.

This time it really was over, for good, and he knew it.

Two years.

After a few minutes, he forced himself to sit up, wipe his face, and shuffle to the washroom.

The shower, detecting his scent, activated helpfully as he entered.

Everything he'd thought he wanted in life seemed suddenly colorless and exhausting; every avenue of optimism lead to nowhere. Nothing could counter the joyless fugue he saw ahead.

Geren sighed, kicking off his underwear—even his sweat smelled of stress.

Resting his back against the little bathroom's tiny vanity, he dragged claws through his beige bellyfur and watched the water spatter hopelessly against the shower's back wall.

Leaning further back, he pulled his tail up between his legs to stroke through its shag and smooth a few tangles from its tip.

It had been nearly a month since he'd had a trim, and all his fur was beginning to follow its natural contours.

He didn't care much; ungroomed fur wasn't considered professional, but he didn't think it looked bad on him.

Still, it was definitely making his scent stronger.

He released his tail and rummaged through the supply cubby, nudging his roommate's oils out of the way to get to his brush set.

What would the future look like alone? It was a thought that he hadn't seriously considered since he'd become involved with Alain.

After a few minutes of aimless grooming, he threw his brushes back into their bag, tossing it onto the counter and deactivated the shower unit without ever stepping in.

He wasn't in the mood to feel clean.

He ran his claws through his slightly-shaggy hair, then tossed his bag back into the cubby and exited into the common area.

On the little shelf above the locker in his bunk glowed a picture of a happy skunk wrapping his arms around a grinning, fey coyote. It had been captured barely a year ago on vacation to Hope's capital city.

Geren smirked weakly in fond recollection of the night that had followed. The dinner had been digested, the libations were barely memorable, and the scenery, while pretty, was safely ensconced in picture . . . but that night—

the start of a half-week-long journey of dazed intimacy in the arms of Alain—was one he would never forget.

An unpalatable sense of loss rushed over him and his stomach clenched, memories turning to acid. He swallowed back nausea and adrenaline as his sympathetic nervous system finally caught up to the realization that he would never have that again.

Growling a light growl that was half anger, half pain, he swept the picture off the shelf and jammed it into the reclamation chute. With increasing anguish, he began to do the same with all of the little trinkets that had marked their affection, starting with the little gifts and moving up to the big ones. Even the stylish, expensive jumpsuit that Alain had presented him with a mere half-year ago, a gift for the first anniversary of his employment, went in after only a moment's hesitation.

Every single thing he threw in caused him an almost physical pain . . . but pain, at least, seemed an appropriate emotion, and there was no stopping.

He slammed the chute shut on the last of it, then slammed it again, shaking the thin, cheap wall. With an anguished groan, he sank back against his bedframe and closed his eyes, fighting off recollections of the happier times and barely holding back tears.

Before long, the soft buzz of his pre-shift alarm caught his attention, and he reached up to silence it, brushing his paw across the pad. With a little shake of his head, he swung to his feet and dug his work coveralls from his locker cubicle, trying to force his mind away from his personal life and focus his work-shift routine.

Work, his father had often lectured him, would be his one reliable friend. 'People will come and go,' the gruff coyote had often said, always in the same tone, 'but treat it right, and your career will always be there for you. Show up early, work hard, keep your head down.'

Geren found a sad little unbidden smile shifting his lips at the memory of the man's words; gently, he touched two digits to the center of his forehead in salute, closing his eyes for a moment.

True or not, at the very least his job would divert him from his personal life for a time. Besides, his whole team was due for another seniority raise within the week, so the atmosphere should be festive.

Perhaps he'd go to one of the factory lounges and try to brush the rust off of his social skills.

Reminded of the fact that he was now single, he knelt on his bed to dig through his locker until he found a dusty little black jewelry box. Into it went the lone silver stud from his right ear that had marked him as unavailable; out came the three for his left—single, looking for either gender.

He'd just finished sliding the last one into his ear with trembling paws when he heard someone brush through the door behind him.

Peeking around the half-wall surrounding his bunk, he found his roommate settling a big duffel bag at the foot of his own bed.

"Hey Luri. What're you doing home?"

The otter glanced his way, then shucked his jacket. "Hey-hey. You awake already? I'm off on a medical— 'nother rash, losing fur. They're trying to figure what I was exposed to."

"Ah, that sucks."

"Yeah. Kinda itchy, too, but they gave me some cream for it." The otter tossed his badge on the table. "So hey, did you hear the news?"

"Mm?" Geren tilted his head, rising to his feet and zipping his coveralls. "What news?"

"About the Jordan Continent thing this morning? And all the riots in Pistar?" Luri spoke quickly, irritatingly excited.

7

Geren leaned against the half wall, draping his arm over it. "Eh. You know how I feel about local politics. I just came here to work, that's all."

"Oh c'mon . . . this is pretty big stuff. The locals are real unhappy down there. Not just there, either . . ."

"Ehh." Geren repeated dismissively. "They're on a central world, at least. Guaranteed rights, standard of living, medical care, that sort of thing. I just don't think biting the helping hand of government will help, you know? Work within the system, don't just riot. But what do I know? Anyway, I have my own wreck of a life to worry about."

"Yah?" Luri shifted subjects, looking concerned. "How's shakes?"

"Oh . . . could be a lot better." Geren lifted his head to grin sadly up to Luri, tilting to display his ear. "I have some . . . personal issues."

The otter glanced at his face for the briefest moment before his eyes found Geren's earstuds and his expression fell.

"Ahh. Man, for real? He actually did it."

"Guess it's no surprise to you?"

"Wish I could say it was, Gerr. Scuttlebutt had you two done a couple days ago."

Geren sank back against his bunk with a growl. "Well feck. Nobody told me."

"You wouldn't have believed it."

"Maybe not. I don't understand it, I really don't. Last time we spoke, he insisted there would always be room for me. He always said 'always,' like there was no doubt."

"Yeah man, you said. Sorry."

"I mean . . . he just dumped me over the terminal. Wouldn't even answer my calls or messages, but since Brodie left himself logged in again, I used his account. Alain picked it right up. So my only companion for two years was going to just . . . ignore me until I went away?"

Luri exhaled a sympathetic sigh, leaning back against the kitchenette chiller. "That's tough. You know, his new boy is upper management. Those guys, man . . . especially lately. I heard some bad stuff—the rumors are flying right now."

"You and your rumors." Geren snorted derisively, hearing in his own voice a hint of his father's disdain for people who let themselves be caught up in gossip. He smiled sourly at his roommate. "They're always wrong, anyway."

"The one about you and Alain wasn't."

"Ouch."

"And the one about them breaking up CEMTA, that one wasn't wrong either." Luri folded his arms across his chest.

"Well, those guys were useless anyway."

"Man, whatever." The otter rolled his eyes. "They were our only employee reps. Not like they could do much, but they tried."

"The company may not be perfect, but they try to do right by us, and I trust them. It's just like my dad said, though . . . lotsa workers would rather just stir things up, and that's all CEMTA did. Me, I just show up, do my job, come back home, and ignore all the rumors."

"And the news, and politics, and current events . . . yeah, man, I know. But sometimes it's important, you know? Maybe you should listen up a bit more."

"It wasn't always what CEMTA said—I got to hear the real story from Alain most of the time, you know." A rush of loss spiraled through Geren, and he turned away, feeling genuinely sick to his stomach. He licked his lips, feeling saliva building up in his mouth.

Luri kicked off his boots and knelt beside Geren. "Yeah? And you still trust all those things he said?"

"Good point."

"Bud, all you ever talked about for weeks is saving your relationship, but I dunno man." The otter raked Geren with an odd look. "I dunno about that skunk or his new beau. Might wanna pick up your head, perk those big ears of yours, and stop focusing on him for a bit."

"Yeah." Geren wiped his muzzle with the back of a paw and swallowed, trying to tame his digestive tract. "Well, I don't want to think about anything right now. I'm gonna get down there early and get my favorite lifter."

"Aw man." Luri made a face, the fine fur around his nose wrinkling up in disgust. "Lifters? Gotta pay your dues, though, right?"

"That's what they say. Living the dream, or whatever. I bet you that when we're both chief reac engineers, we look back on this stuff and miss it."

"Yeah . . . yeah, maybe. No, you know what? Naw. Naw, man. I won't miss the leaks, dumps, represses, depresses, patches on top of patches, all to save the cost of doing it right. I sure won't miss the chemical burns, thermal burns, workers going on 'permanent leave,' having to shack up with a coworker or two—no offense. I won't miss the fires, the 'mystery foam,' itching myself to sleep, getting paid less than the cleaners . . . and I sure as hell won't miss almost losing six limbs a day to those junk-tastic lifters."

Geren stepped into his boots, clamping them around his calves and cinching them down. He stretched, then leaned against the doorframe with a snort. "You know, I actually enjoy 'em."

"You're such a company man," Luri laughed.

"Eh. I've never thought they were too dangerous. I find 'em relaxing. Sometimes running reac is just constant mental gymnastics . . . and mystery foam." Geren smirked, but it slid away quickly. "Today I get to shut my brain off and stop being an engineer, or . . . eh. Hey, any interest in the lounge later?"

"Now there's an idea. Yeah. Definitely." The otter grinned slyly. "Kory might want to go, too. I'll ask her when she's off-shift."

"Yeah . . . that sounds nice."

"She likes you, man. I know she does. Maybe give her a chance, huh?"

Geren slung his pack over his shoulder and forced a grin.

"Sure. Tonight, then. Drinks are on me."

Making his way out of his little bunkroom, Geren tromped towards the nearest pod nexus, gazing listlessly down through the angled windows to watch the activity below.

The dormitory section was located at the top tier of the multi-kilometer-long factory in which he worked; the catwalks that connected the bunkrooms overlooked the factory floor nearly two hundred meters down.

Settled on the edge of Fenna City, ostensibly the planet's largest city and the planetary capital, it was Cerion's biggest plant on Fonaci. So large was it in scale that its construction had to account for the curvature of the planet, the workers were often told.

A self-contained city, it only imported food and power; everything else was built or made in-house. Everything he needed—food, social time, shopping—was available 'downstairs' within the confines of the plant.

Even the shuttle to the transfer station launched from within the factory perimeter.

While they weren't strictly prohibited from venturing outside the factory grounds, almost everyone followed the company recommendation to stay within.

The city outside was rough, they were warned.

A hiss from one of the nexus tubes announced an arriving pod, and he shuffled over to it. Inside, he selected the work floor drop point near the lifter bays rather than the usual office-side exit.

He could check in after picking up his favorite lifter, then grab a container of verti to get him through until the first break.

Satisfied with his plan, he stepped out of the pod and headed for the lifters.

So early was he that not a soul was to be found on the loading floor—even the dispatcher's station was empty, and the work lights were off. He worked his way past the growing stack of crates, angling towards #39 lifter hold.

#39 had always treated him well.

Oddly, when he tried to check out the twelve ton machine from its bay, the terminal made an irritating noise, but the gate remained shut.

He rubbed his chin and frowned, walking over to the next bay. This one had one of the newer-style security systems, but it too rejected his credentials, flashing an angry 'security violation' message on the screen.

"Great," he grumbled to himself. "Today, of all days, I show up early, and the security network is down."

He pulled a portable comm from the loader bay locker and selected the support contact.

Heavy bootfalls across the depot caught his attention, and he looked up to see his shift supervisor jogging towards him, datapad clutched in his hand and a scowl on his face.

He straightened and lifted a paw to the equine in greeting, dropping the comm back into its holder. "Hey, boss."

"Geren!" Ehrse seemed unusually wary as he slowed. "What are you doing?"

Geren arched an eyebrow, perking his ears at the strange question. "Well, it's my day on lifters. Just came down a bit early, but the access system is broken. Again. Everything alright?"

"More or less." Ehrse shifted on his feet, holstering his pad. "No lifters today. We're having a supervisor's meeting. Just finishing it up now, in fact. Come up and have some verti."

Geren nodded, perplexed; his personal troubles had destroyed his attention span for weeks. He couldn't visualize the schedule, but he'd been certain that this shift was lifters.

There certainly seemed to be enough sitting around to have three lifter shifts in a row.

He followed the two-meter tall Ehrse, falling in step and surreptitiously straightening his coveralls.

"Hey, so what are we going to do about all the backlog on the floor?"

"We've got this new mag lift system they're going to be testing out this month." Ehrse spoke over his shoulder without looking back. "It's a new thing for us, straight from Brynton. Goes right along with that reac retrofit you've been working on."

"Oh. Wow, ok . . ."

A group of workers was engaged in setting up orange and white barriers around the main pod drop, cordoning off the work floor. One of them pushed the fencing open as they approached, beckoning them through.

"Is it dangerous?" Geren asked, watching the worker locking the gate behind them. It seemed a bit much, especially given the fast-and-loose view the company had on safety.

Ehrse grunted noncommittally and wouldn't meet his eye.

Geren was confused and slightly suspicious, but suspicion quickly began to dominate; his boss was always painfully honest and direct.

Something bad must have happened, he realized; there was no other explanation for Ehrse's behavior.

He perked his ears at the sound of his shiftmates coming down the walk from the nearby pod stop; they were laughing and joking, though their voices fell to muffled surprise as they found themselves directed away from the work floor by another set of workers.

"Hey people! We're meeting in the break room," Ehrse spoke loudly, waving for them to follow him.

"Was there another accident?" Geren lowered his voice.

Ehrse seemed edgy, and made no response.

Geren's suspicion began to change to fear—something was actively not right; even after past injury accidents, Ehrse generally defaulted to indulging in his fluent invective, rather than silence.

As he approached the open archway, his nose caught the scent of perfume, and he felt his hackles rise further.

Something was very wrong.

Some animal sense made him want to pull back.

The black-coated equine ushered him inside and followed him through the doorway.

Six people in formal attire were sitting at a broad table where the refreshments normally sat, and there was no verti in sight. Six burly security guards were leaning against the far wall, most of them watching him. One, a massively-built russet wolf, seemed to stare at him with unguarded interest and a strange, smug little grin.

Geren stopped two paces inside, then took a half step back, instinctively wanting to retreat from this tableau; he was stopped by a firm grip on his shoulder, and looked up to discover another pair of guards flanking the door behind him.

"Ah, our first customer." An otter at the table, dressed in crisp clothing wholly unsuitable for the factory floor he was on, spoke up in a cheery voice. He slid a datapad out of a little box and rested it in front of Geren. "Chip please. Are you contingent?"

"Ah, what?" Baffled and frightened, Geren turned back to Erhse, catching his breath at his boss's strange, suffused expression.

"Geren . . ." Erhse lowered his voice. "The retrofits . . . we're cutting staff."

Geren felt himself go numb—he almost couldn't breathe. A susurration carried out the door behind him, building in little bursts as the message was passed along, and he stared up at Ehrse; realizing his muzzle was slightly open, he closed it with a snap. "But . . . me, sir?"

Ehrse looked unhappy. "You're a damn good engineer, and a good worker. I'm sorry, son. These people here will help you with the forms."

"But . . ."

The equine held up a big hand.

"Whatever it is, ask them. They're here to help."

"Engineer? Not contingent, then!" The otter dragged his attention away as Ehrse retreated. "Geren, is it? Ah, yes, here you are. Reaction control engineer, originally from Alaran. Chipped?"

"Yeah, of course I am." Geren held out his paw, his pulse rapid, breathing shallow.

This couldn't be happening.

The otter lifted a chip scanner to scan his palm, then nudged the datapad toward him. "Your severance documents. Please authenticate your key to sign them."

Feeling lightheaded, he tapped out his passcode, and the otter began working at his terminal. There wasn't even a chair to sink into. From behind, he heard soft noises, and turned to see his bewildered-looking shiftmates filtering in behind.

"So . . ." Geren murmured, then cleared his throat. "We're not being transferred or anything? Like, to another plant?"

"I'm afraid not." The otter smiled a condescending little smile, then sat up straight, tapping one last time at the workscreen in front of him. "There, that should do it. Your bunk will be packed for you at no additional charge, and you may take delivery in the mall outside the main entrance. There will be a series of lines by name—the 'G's will be divided into the first two letters."

"Wait . . ." Geren couldn't believe his ears. "Slow down . . . you're telling me that I can't even pack my own things?"

"That's right." The otter nodded smoothly. "Terminated employees have a habit of engaging in criminal activity, so it's really for your own protection."

"Are . . . what?" Geren was dumbfounded, and his voice faltered. "Criminal activity? But I—"

"On this datapad is an affirmation of your termination." The otter interrupted cheerfully, as if he'd said nothing. "Your final payroll has been processed—we've taken your account, deducted your living expenses, commissary, TC and miscellaneous. As per Cerion SPD 8281, the sum has been settled to Fonaci istaks and a token for release has been placed on this credit chit. If you need a relocation loan to go off-planet—which, given your balance, I do strongly suggest—talk to Melody down at the end there. The company is prepared to offer very competitive rates with reasonable repayment terms. She can even set up a deferred-interest plan for a nominal fee."

"Relocation loan? This . . . is this a joke?" Geren could hear echoes of his disbelief beginning to circulate as the shocked line of workers reacted to similar statements. "The contract I signed . . . Cerion guaranteed relocation back—I made sure of that before I came out! It was guaranteed!"

"Oh dear. You do read your T&C changes, don't you?"

"You can't change something like that without telling us!" Geren stared, mouth dry as he pictured the bolus of barely-structured jargon that formed the company manual with its daily updates, and genuine fear began to take hold. "Anyway . . . it shouldn't matter! The contract—"

"—was amendable at Cerion's discretion, Geren." The otter held up a single digit, tone didactically disapproving. "Which was stated right there on the contract you countersigned! Goodness. We even put it in bold. You're delaying your shiftmates!"

"But . . ."

The otter held up a hand, then slid the credit chit across to him, setting it on the little datapad and giving it a little pat. "Just a few more things. Due to the short notice, the company has generously extended an offer to stay for up to a week at a reduced rate in Hotel Niyoz, to which you will be provided complimentary transportation."

"You're not even sending us up to the transfer station?"

"No. However, should you wish to transfer off-planet, there is a ticket counter at the Niyoz."

"But the shuttle—"

"The company shuttle is only for company employees."

"But I—I—just like that . . . ?"

"Yes." Decisive and absolute. "You will be transported to the factory foyer once everyone has finished processing out. There you will exit to the mall, collect your belongings, and board a private bus to the hotel Niyoz. Make no attempt to re-enter the factory perimeter—anyone caught in the exclusion zone inside the outer ring road is subject to arrest."

Geren felt a cool wariness descend along his spine, displacing a bit of his initial shock as the reality of the situation began to nibble at his psyche.

The otter tapped his screen, then looked back up, as if reading from notes. "Ah, yes. Lastly, please stay between the outer ring road and third street. That area is called 'the grey,' and it is considered relatively safe. If your presence is recorded beyond sixth street, you may not be permitted off-planet."

"What?" he asked, startled into speech. "What about right to roam?"

"That concept is not recognized here." Irritation once again crept in to the otter's voice. "Now, really, we have a very busy day ahead of us—this isn't easy, you know, and you're making it much harder for all of us with these silly questions."

"Oh really? I'm terribly sorry." Anger, slow to rise, was at last beginning to seep in to replace the numb shock. "None of this is legal, you know."

The otter's eyes narrowed. "I can personally assure you that this is all completely legal under Fonaci corporate law. You're on Fonaci, in case you hadn't noticed, and Cerion is a corporation. Now, did you want to speak with Melody about one of our relocation plans, or shall I refer you to our security?"

"You . . ." Geren growled, dazed but certain he didn't want to be talked into signing any more contracts with Cerion. "You guys are scum, doing this to us like this."

"Please step into the back room to finish processing out, sir." The otter spoke curtly, instantly icy. "I have treated you with complete respect, but verbal abuse will not be tolerated."

"This is surreal," Geren found himself muttering aloud, uncertain whether to hurl more ineffective invective or to slink off with his tail between his legs.

From the looks on the faces of those around him, and the rising timbre of conversation, his was not an uncommon sentiment.

The otter was clearly done with him, however; he lifted his paw, and the burly, semi-armored wolf who had been eying him was there in two smooth strides.

To his shock, the wolf actually clamped a paw around his arm, pushing him towards the back of the room.

Geren jerked away from the wolf's touch and stepped back, baring his teeth.

"Hey! Touch me again, and I'll call the police. I'll have you arrested. For assault!"

The wolf rolled his eyes in disgust, then stepped forward, looming over him. "I *am* the police, and if you don't step through that curtain I *will* assault you."

Geren stood for a moment, feeling many eyes upon him. The wolf looked to be upwards of a hundred and thirty kilograms, with an array of evil tools on his belt and a relaxed readiness that gave him the air of an experienced fighter.

Geren had been in one fight in his life, as a pup.

He'd lost.

Shoulders square, he turned and walked through the curtain as directed, trying to keep what poise he could despite the malevolent presence behind him.

A large rack of plain brown coveralls was labeled in two sizes—medium and large. A display sign above the rack demanded the return of company uniforms, ID cards, access tokens and tools; bins were arrayed to receive them.

"Change." The wolf's deep voice carried hints of annoyance as he stepped through behind him.

"Will I be charged for this, too?" Geren spat the question, gesturing to the coveralls.

"Hell if I know," the wolf growled, "but you're not leaving until you change."

Geren bit back a retort, unclipping his badge and throwing it into a bin. Straightening up, he shucked his boots and leg pads, then stripped off the form-fitting one-piece factory uniform he'd donned minutes before and threw it into a different bin.

He could feel the guard's eyes on him, and practically feel his breath on the back of his neck. Angry and frustrated, he jerked away from the wolf's proximity and yanked out the bottommost of the 'medium' coveralls, scattering the rest across the floor.

A powerful blow to his back slammed him against the wall, and he slid down to land atop the scattered garments, rolling over to stare up at the wolf in shock.

"Don't fuck around or I'll beat the life out of you," the guard snarled coolly, looming over him. "We get bonuses for that. Highlight of the job for me, so go ahead."

Geren dropped his gaze to the floor, angry but impotent. Without another word, he carefully stood and slid into the much-too-large brown coverall, zipping its single zipper up to his chest and closing the cavernous cuffs around his ankles and wrists.

He reached for his boots, but the guard took him firmly by the shoulder and lifted him back up, pulling him away from them.

"Company property. Out. You taking a loan?"

"No," Geren snapped. "I—hey!"

The wolf spun him around and shoved him unceremoniously back through the curtain, hot on his heels. A paw closed on his scruff, and the din of the room fell to an uncertain hush; he felt the horrified stares of everyone on him as he was marched back out to the factory floor.

A fat little automated transport shuttle was settling just outside the breakroom.

"Don't take it too personal," the wolf muttered in his ear, a bit of amusement sneaking into his voice. "Keeps the others in line. Sets a tone. Cools 'em down. All that stuff."

Geren grunted and stared straight ahead. Once the shuttle had come to rest and the door opened, the wolf pushed him inside. He sank into the first row and curled up against the window, facing away.

To his surprise, the wolf settled in beside him.

"What, are you my personal guard?"

The wolf grinned a strange little grin, leaning into his space. "If you want me to be, cute stuff."

Geren shrank further into his seat, retreating into confusion. "Wha? Excuse me?"

"I'll take that as a maybe," the guard said with a smirk. He reached in and very gently took hold of Geren's coveralls, opening the zipper a little further. Pulling a little note card from his pocket, he slid it in, pushing it down past the coyote's chestfur and leaning close.

"All that before was mostly show," he whispered, whiskers tickling Geren's ear. "I can be a lot nicer. And if you stay with me, I won't gouge you like they will in the Niyoz. Just need a bit of housework and a bit of company."

Geren wrinkled his nose; the wolf's breath smelled slightly of ethanol, but otherwise he just smelled very much like wolf.

It wasn't wholly unpleasant, and a little shiver coursed through him.

He flinched away and shook his head, as much to dispel the momentary vulnerability as in response to the wolf's suggestion.

"Definitely not. No. What kind of person do you think I am?"

A look akin to faint disappointment transited the wolf's face, but it faded so quickly that Geren wondered if he'd imagined it. He looked over his shoulder then eased back out of his seat, far more limber than his size would suggest. "Hey, suit yourself, but I was tasked to watch out for you. Can't do it if you don't let me."

"I don't need watching out for," Geren muttered, turning his head to pointedly stare out the window. "Especially not from somebody like you."

The wolf snorted softly, leaning back into the row. "Well, you got my contact there—use it before you get in trouble, not after."

"Trouble?" Geren lifted his head, looking over his shoulder, spurred to ask. "What sort of trouble could I possibly get in? I'm getting off-planet on the first ship."

The wolf's expression grew earnest, and he nodded. "Good plan. Don't see so much in here, but they're in a bad way out there . . . this city most of all. It's beyond crime— the locals are about feral." He glanced up as the first cluster of workers was escorted onto the shuttle, then turned back and leaned close, resting a paw on Geren's thigh. "Listen, anything happens, you don't make it out, you run out of funds, you just call me. I'll take care of you."

Geren shuddered, staring at the wolf's misplaced paw as if it were diseased. "I don't need to be taken care of, either," he growled quietly, compressing even further down and wanting to shudder away. "I can take care of myself."

The wolf's eyes glinted, and he smirked a condescending little smirk down at him. "Uh huh. Name's Lapis. Change your mind, call me."

Geren looked away entirely, curling around his knees as the paw was withdrawn. He heard Lapis move off, but didn't look up or uncurl until all of his shiftmates had entered, and the shuttle had closed its door and begun to move.

More than a dozen workers sat in utter silence, and a pall of shock hung over the lot.

Tasked to watch out for him? Geren felt slightly ill. No—he had a good idea of what that wolf really wanted, and he wanted no part of it.

His thoughts swung to Alain, and clutched at his belly—he wasn't sure he ever wanted to be in any sort of relationship again.

He turned his eyes up toward the administrative offices, wondering what his former boyfriend would do when he found out.

Terminated.

His father had always spoken of terminated workers like an excised disease—underperforming, peculating, insubordinate or otherwise generally bad. People were power, he'd said; you never got rid of the good ones.

Geren hung his head in shame, resting his face in his paws, hair hanging over them.

His first job, and he'd been terminated just two years in.

At least his parents weren't around to know.

The transport lifted a few meters, then began to slide forward, and Geren looked up again to stare out the window.

From the work floor, the small transport continued to gain altitude, turning and headed out across the #3 assembly section, rising to pass over hundreds of hectares of automated machinery dancing its perpetual dance of creation. Down there was his whole life—he knew every section, every pipe, and how to get to every conduit and check valve.

He stared out, glassy-eyed, as they moved quickly beyond his domain to parts of the factory he'd never seen, but his curiosity was diminished to nothing.

It was no longer his to care about.

Staying high over the fab and assembly sections, the shuttle gradually arced left, sweeping half a kilometer away from the giant admin inbuilding lit by dancing orange light from the skylights in the factory roof far above. He could see a little garden park on its upper deck, all synthetic sunlight and real greenery, and fancy offices, appointed with every amenity.

Somewhere in there, Alain would be waiting for Merrine to come home. Would Alain ask Merrine about his shift and tell him about their conversation? Would they go out to the executive-wing restaurant for a nice dinner and toast to their future?

Would they ever think of him again?

Geren wiped moist eyes with his paw, trying to slow his breathing and not embarrass himself further.

He wouldn't sob . . . he'd just stay afloat, and keep swimming until he found land.

As the transit approached the far end of the factory, it slowed and began to descend, and Geren pressed his face against the window to look down.

He'd never been near this end below the twentieth level, where the company shuttle launched; it mostly appeared to be automated system management and waste processing for biologicals support, judging by the configuration and color-coding of the piping.

At the terminus, the transport turned between two tremendous pipes and began a descent, sinking through a staged series of airlocks. Eventually it emerged from the final airlock into an open atrium; below, but quickly coming into view, was a well-staffed guardpost and the factory's main gate, which the transport settled just behind.

Another squad of security was arranged in a loose formation near the landing spot.

A murmur of concern rippled through the little transit, and he stood with the rest, catching his very first glimpse of the city outside the factory.

It was not encouraging.

Tenements of all sizes huddled together in all directions to form huge, stark, ugly shapes. In the distance, tall buildings formed lightless silhouettes against the orange sky; sleet pelted from the greasy, flat false dawn onto a filthy, colorless amber-lit promenade packed with all manners of traffic, from throngs of pedestrians to transits and cargo barges.

A bitterly cold, wet stench met them head-on as they filed out, and dingy faces of the locals turned to watch the exodus from behind hooded cloaks.

Geren's nose sampled the scents of the street and he felt ill; sewage and chemical combustion byproducts, the corruption and the filth of urban decay, the smell of burning and the pong of wet civilization all instantly impinged upon his sense of cleanliness and the order his life had known.

He stood and stared, wondering how this world could possibly meet any of the central worlds standards . . . and this was the inner section? The section they weren't even permitted to return to?

How much worse was it in 'the grey'? Or beyond the sixth street checkpoint?

It was too much stimulus; the world was much too large, and dirty, and it was dizzying. He tried to shut it out and dampen his awareness of it, but succeeded only enough to stand with the rest and dumbly make his way to the table where their belongings were to be claimed.

Checking through his sack, when at last it was presented to him, he was dismayed to find that his datapad was missing. He looked up to find the guard behind the table staring straight at his face.

"My pad—"

"Your pad had proprietary company information on it."

"Of course it did!" Geren barked, attracting the attention of several sets of ears. "I didn't exactly know this was happening, or I would have purged it."

"Watch your tone," the guard growled, stiffening and resting his paw on his baton. "You can file an appeal to have it wiped and returned, for a fee. Now move along."

Geren caught motion out of the corner of his eye and sucked in a little breath as he found himself bracketed by silent security.

"Any more questions?" one of the pair asked, baton out and resting in the crook of his arm.

"No," Geren muttered. He clutched his mostly-empty sack to his chest and turned away. The others were gathering at the side of a dingy armored ground transport, and he scuttled over, heart beating rapidly at the menace he felt from the security staff.

Meekly stepping into line, he lowered his gaze to stare at the bare heels of the worker in front of him, feeling more alone and directionless than he had since the day he'd been told that his father had gone missing.

His paw crept up to touch Lapis' card where it rested beneath his coveralls, and he thought back on the wolf's comments.

He bit his lip, clenching his paws to stop them from shaking.

No.

This was a setback, but not the end.

He would keep his head down, he would stay focused, and he would survive this.

Everything would turn out fine—he was a licensed and trained industrial reaction engineer, with top marks and two years of experience, and he was still at the beginning of what promised to be a long, productive career.

He had almost a year of pay saved up and, without Alain or his job, he had nothing holding him to Fonaci.

It was freeing, in a way.

With a shake of his head, he forced himself to look away from the squalor that surrounded him, baring his teeth in a determined grimace.

The plight of this planet wasn't his—step zero would be to escape and regroup. His savings should be enough to live for a standard month or so on Ramesan, and Ramesan had basic income and guaranteed state jobs, should he prove unable to find something more lucrative in the private sector.

He closed his eyes and wrested his emotions back. He'd get off this planet, and when he was back on his feet, he'd do better than a dirty job with a third-rate employer.

Ramesan it was.

"Ramesan?" The old opossum at the ticket desk of the Hotel Niyoz pulled down his glasses, looking down at Geren over the rims. "You sure about that?"

Geren tilted his head, taken aback. "Well, yes. Is that a problem?"

"Well, no. No, it's not a *problem*. Not if you've got the funds for it."

He dropped his chit into the reader, paw trembling slightly from the accumulation of stress, then nodded up at the agent. "Yeah. We're not locals, you know— we were all just laid off from Cerion."

The opossum fixed him with a long, unfathomable stare, then turned back to his terminal.

"For one?"

"Yes," Geren sighed, thinking of his last trip and how much more promise life had held then. "Yes. Yes, it's just me from now on."

"Ah, me. Well, next available liner will be a little over one hundred twenty-three thousand more than what you've got on this here."

Geren's breath froze for half a moment, then he stepped forward, tilting his head. "Wait, wait—istaks?"

"Istaks. That's what we use here, is istaks."

Geren rattled his claws firmly on the counter in a staccato beat, looking at the back of the agent's terminal as if he could see through it. "No, look, I just want the lowest fare, not premier. Even lounge seating is fine."

"Kid, that's already basic class." The ticket agent turned his terminal toward Geren, pointing out the fare line with its complicated code and associated price.

"Uh . . ." Geren glanced back over his shoulder at the glum line of workers behind him, noticing for the first time that most held red relocation loan chits. He gulped down a tiny thread of panic, resting a paw on his churning belly. "Ok. Ok, look . . . just . . . find me the cheapest within a week. Two weeks, even."

"Well, now, that does bring it down a bit. We're looking at . . . hm . . . one hundred five thousand istaks. So this here card is short by about eighty thou. Got a relocation card for me?"

"That's . . . a hundred and five? That's crazy!" Geren rested a paw on his head, aghast. "This chit has gotta be at least a year's pay! How much is an istak worth?"

"Oh, let me think, here. I'd say . . . 'bout one istak. You know, plus or minus."

Geren snapped his jaw shut and glowered.

"Welp, kiddie," the opossum seemed almost gleeful, lips pulling back in a nasty sneer to reveal stained teeth. "Looks as though you ain't goin' to Ramesan any time soon, now, doesn't it? What, you think twenty thousand istaks is a lot? Enough for a pumped up factory worker at Cerion, I s'pose, living on your factory credit. You're not just some dirt-bag local, after all. Well you're right, twenty thou is a lot to us locals . . . not so's you can do much with it . . . but it still ain't enough to get you to Ramesan."

"But I—I just went to Hope last year, and for two of us it was only nine thousand!" Geren could feel the eyes of the others on him, as if they finally had started listening to the conversation, and felt himself flush beneath his fur.

"You may not have noticed, up in your cozy factory, but out here in the real Fonaci, we're ruined. Thanks to you people. You got local currency, but our currency ain't worth anything to the rest of the universe anymore."

"I . . . but . . ." Geren felt dizzy, short of breath.

"Guess what? You're a local now." The ticket agent smirked down at him, then turned the terminal back around, pushing his glasses back up. "Let me help you out, one local to another. There is one world that you can get to with your money, and that's Brynton. Want me to book you a ticket, sir?"

"Good god no!" Geren felt a visceral shudder run through him at the mention of that planet. "This is unreal."

"Well, then. If you ain't buyin' a ticket, stop wastin' my time." The agent smacked his paw on the table and turned away pointedly to look at the person behind him. "Can I help whoever's next?"

Dazed, Geren removed his chip, picked up his bag, and stepped away from the ticket counter.

He had no idea what else to do.

A large 'Cerion' sign posted beside the counter pointed down to a yellow line taped to the floor. Putting one foot before the other, Geren followed it down a hallway, through a set of swinging doors and across the lobby of the hotel.

The Niyoz had clearly once been a luxury establishment, but everything had decayed to, at best, shabby and worn, the once-bright colors faded almost to greyscale monotony. A grand fireplace was cordoned off by a leaning sheet of metal, and the banister on the winding stair that arched over it had broken—decades ago, from the looks of it—and been replaced with a simple metal perimeter fence railing.

The stone floor to the ticket counter and rotunda, a fine mural in some happier day, bore giant cracks, repaired patches and missing chunks. What must have been a lovely scene was thrown into disheveled, scraped chaos, coated in grunge and strewn with sand and trash.

A cool breeze from the direction of the kitchen carried with it a stale, fetid odor that reminded Geren of the cafeteria food at the community school he'd attended as a youngling, with a slight twinge of rancidity.

Even less hungry than before, he walked the taped yellow line as it led him up to the guest services counter, feeling heavier with every step.

A stoat behind the counter sauntered over, extending his paw for Geren's credit chit.

"You're one of the Cerion lot, ay?" The stoat slid the chit into a little reader after Geren tendered it. "Chipped? Paw here and authenticate. Thank you. Give me one moment."

Geren leaned on the counter and avoided eye contact.

"Ah, here we go. Yep, this looks like you. Well, we do got a room block for you lot, so that's good. Cerion . . . so you guys all just termed?"

"Yeah," Geren said, looking up at last. He rested his paws on the counter, leaning forward. "Yeah, all of us. I thought I was going to go off-planet, but I'm stuck."

"Oh, oh . . . I'm sorry about that, my friend." The stoat reached over and touched his paw softly, and Geren resisted the urge to flinch away as he noticed that the clerk's white-furred face was covered in little white furless scars. "This is all you got?"

"Yeah," Geren sighed. "I thought it would be a lot. It was a year's savings."

"Cerion, they're not so nice." The stoat pulled his paw back, shaking his head in sympathy. "Don't even warn you, ay? Then cash you out in istaks. So much inflation on the istak this year, and that's what they give, ay? And our rates, they're normed to shipping rates on the Alari standard, so . . . Istak's almost worth nothing. Nobody uses istaks."

Geren winced. "Are there any, uh, other hotels nearby that take istaks?"

"This is really the only operating hotel in the city, sir. And like I said, nobody uses istaks, really. We don't even get 'em for working here . . . we're just here 'cause they let us live in here. You still want a room?"

Geren gazed down mutely at the deep cracks in the hardwood counter.

"Yeah, unless you have any suggestions for me."

"Wish I did. Let me see what I can do, room-wise."

"The only hotel in the city, though? The whole city? Really?"

The stoat glanced up, then looked back down to the terminal. "You haven't really been out much, have you?"

Geren shook his head and turned to watch the dazed group shuffling over from the ticket counter. It hadn't only been his shiftmates, he noticed—his whole department appeared to have been hit hard. Another busload was filing through the atrium to stand in the ticket counter queue.

Quite a few of his coworkers looked as though they'd been kicked out of bed mid-slumber, and the few couples were clinging together for mutual support. A stray stab of acid bitterness sank into his gut, and he exhaled through his teeth, turning back to the stoat, who looked up.

"Sorry, my friend, but for this room here you're looking at about six thousand a week, plus taxes and fees. That's the best rate I can get you. I promise, I tried. At least this one it's a private room with a bathroom. This is the best of the block, though—it even has a working terminal!" The stoat sounded almost cheerful, as if he were offering some great luxury. "Ok with you?"

Done with being surprised, Geren simply nodded and signed the form with a tap of his paw.

"What if I leave early? Can I do that?"

"Oh yes, sir." The clerk brightened, tapping at his terminal. "Charge is by the day, so leaving before noon means no more charges. Room's yours now. #314."

"Thanks," Geren sighed. "Anything else?"

The stoat leaned across the table, gesturing for Geren to come close.

"Don't eat at the restaurant."

Room #314 at the Hotel Niyoz was bigger than his dormitory bunk, but not by much.

It was also significantly filthier.

What luxury amenities the room had once boasted had mostly been destroyed or removed; a bare thermo-resistive light on the wall—archaic as it was—was the only source of illumination, and even the soft synthetic flooring had been ripped up long ago.

All sorts of unsavory sounds penetrated the water- and mold-stained walls, and the room reeked of a composite funk that defied analysis.

He dropped his possessions and collapsed onto the bare bed, perpetually on the verge of tears.

His whole world, his promising start, had been reduced to one sack and credentials which, if one threw in a loaf of bread, would feed him for a day. His life savings were barely enough to keep him alive for the next two weeks.

He had no idea what the level of housing assistance was on the planet, nor how to apply for social programs for food or employment, but he didn't want to have to find out.

He had to get off this planet, back to somewhere safe and sane.

Barely able to hold himself together, he pulled over the room's antiquated terminal, breathing ragged as he fought off sobs. He swiped his paw, tapped his code, tapped 'call,' and selected Alain from the list.

"Alain?" He started before the connection had even finished its handshake, voice shaking. "Alain, there's been—"

"Unauthorized." A large 'X' filled his terminal, and a pleasant, happy synthesized voice accompanied it. "This user has declined future contacts from you. Any further attempt from this ID will be referred to prosecution for harassment. Goodbye."

Geren hissed an inarticulate curse, but it froze in his throat. He pushed back, gaping at the bottom of the terminal display—he had been billed five hundred istaks for the connection fee. Looking at the terminal's legend, he was aghast—all access was billed at the punitive rate of sixty istaks a minute.

He sank back onto his tail, eyes unfocused, in some form of emotional shock that he'd never learned about in school.

After a few minutes, he unzipped his coverall and drew out Lapis' card. It was a simple contact address with a brown stain at the bottom corner.

He stared at it for a few more minutes, then dropped it into his thigh pocket with a small shudder.

Surely not.

Hiding his face in his paws, he curled up in the gritty bed, willing himself to wake up from what must surely be some too-realistic nightmare.

Alain had been pulling away for a long time. It hurt tremendously, but he'd suspected this day was coming, and he'd been as prepared as he could be. But his job, his savings . . . his life?

Unless his fortune changed dramatically, he would very soon be on that ugly street with no home, no money and no income on a world he'd guess as second only to Brynton in its uncharitable handling of its poor.

A little compulsive shudder gripped him. He had heard of layoffs at Cerion before, of course, but they were relatively infrequent, and often couched in terms of improving efficiency by reducing underperforming teams so the rest could grow.

Such stories had always come off as sad but unavoidable, and unlikely to happen to him. He'd never seemed to know anyone directly affected. Worse, like everyone else, he'd always assumed that those so released had been relocated, with severance packages, like they'd been told at signing. He hadn't personally stayed abreast of policy, because he'd never expected to be involuntarily discharged.

He stared at the wall.

Perhaps one of the other cities would be better, he reflected; he didn't want to live here, if what he'd already seen was any indication of how things were . . . although from the sound of things, the whole planet was facing an economic crisis.

Geren jolted upright, struck by the sudden realization that he was being a stubborn idiot—he would be better off taking the relocation loans under any terms.

It was better to be in debt on Ramesan, where he could be drawing currency that was worth something, than temporarily in the black on Fonaci with an account full of worthless istaks.

In fact, once on Ramesan, he realized, he might even be able to have his 'debt' nullified by adjudication as a contract signed under duress.

Hope blooming anew, he sprang out of bed and snatched up his sack, dumping it out. Digging through the pile, he found the severance packet and brought it up on the terminal, trying to read around the dim and broken display to make sense of the archaic and obscure terminology.

He spun through it for a while until at last he found a contact. With only a moment's hesitation at the punitive connection fee, he selected it.

There was a long pause, then the red 'X' faded in once more.

"Unauthorized. Cerion corporation office or factory extensions are off-limits to non-Cerion personnel. Any—"

"Agh!" Geren brought his paw down unnecessarily hard on the terminal, and it went black.

He cringed, prodding at it with a clawtip.

It stayed black.

He yanked out the datastore, then slung the terminal back into its niche and turned to stare at the wall, unseeing.

What was left?

SECOND

NINE HOURS LATER, as the milky opacity of the short day began at last to succumb to the cold, humid pallor of the night, Geren woke.

The weather had continued to turn cold, and ice distorted what little light crept through the little window of his room.

He used the bathroom, then returned to bed, but sleep was gone. After a few hours of tossing and turning in mental and physical discomfort, he gave up on trying.

He had no idea what to do.

Slipping back into his coveralls, he pawed through the rest of his belongings, bereft of guidance. The practical side of him wished that he hadn't thrown away Alain's gift; all he had left to wear aside from the company coveralls was a single pair of pajamas.

He rolled the datastore over in his paws.

Perhaps if he dissected Cerion's numbers, he'd find out what had happened. There had to have been a mistake— there was no way a year's payroll was worth no more than a few weeks in the Niyoz.

Whether he could get it corrected . . .

He shook his head. It was something, at least.

He had to try.

Judging the terminal in his room a lost cause, he shuffled downstairs, settling himself into one of the terminal booths in the lobby.

It became his home for many hours.

At long last, weary to the point of tears, aching from the physical strain of it all, he pushed back from the terminal and removed the datastore, resisting the temptation to smash it on the counter.

He could almost admire the evil beauty of Cerion's work. It was clean, it was precise, it was surgical. Even under the Basic Labor Code, he was pretty sure it would have stood up to scrutiny. Every exploitable piece of language in the contract had been massaged to achieve a result that functioned nothing like how it read at first glance.

Aimless and lost, he shuffled back towards the stairs.

"Gerr!"

Geren looked up in surprise to find one of his coworkers sitting at the otherwise-empty hotel bar, a half-full pink drink in his paw. He padded over to stand beside the short black-furred panther, momentarily happy to see a familiar face.

"Mally . . . what are we going to do?"

"We? Why is it 'we?'" The computer engineer raked him with a suspicious glance. "Figured you'd be gone to Ramesan as soon as this came down—you've got citizenship there, right?"

"I don't have the money, Mal." Geren lowered his voice, as much to keep it steady as to stay unheard. "They screwed me up bad."

Mally gaped at him, cinnamon eyes wide with dismay, then slowly closed his mouth, shaking his head. "Don't . . . please don't tell me you didn't take the loan . . ."

"Look, I didn't know! I thought my savings would be plenty to get me somewhere better, but—"

"How much do you have?"

"After this week is up in this hotel, probably about thirteen thou."

"*Thirteen*?" Mally slammed his drink down on the bar, big teeth flashing in the light. He was actually angry. "You thought that would be enough?"

"I—I," Geren stuttered, taken aback. "I went through all the forms and terms just now . . . I couldn't really figure it out at first, but it looked like they were billing me for everything. Like, everything. Should have had two years of savings in there, but it paid out so low . . . I . . . so I read through it all. I read all the settlement details. They charged me for basic subsistence, Mally. And for my training contract, because I didn't fulfill my five-year term. Even though we were all laid off, they charged me! Almost everything went to that."

"Haven't you been paying attention lately?" Mally growled, more intense than Geren had ever seen him. "That's why they shut down CEMTA! The president sent a message to us about that exact thing, and the company fired the lot of them."

"I didn't read it," Geren admitted guiltily, looking away. "They send out so much stuff . . . and I always thought they were just complaining about nothing, to get concessions later on. My father always told me that if I just kept my head down and worked hard, the company would take care of me."

"Your dad worked for a union shop, under a reputable government!" Mally flexed his claws against the bar, visibly upset. "Cerion's not the same thing. Not at all!"

"So I found out, I guess. But look, even still, I went to Hope last year with Alain, and it only cost a month's credit for the both of us. On a luxury line! How could I have known?"

"Where have you been, kid?" Mally waved his drink around, incredulous. "I mean, really. Where's your head? I can't—look, the economy here . . . it's falling apart. And all that civil unrest in the southern hemisphere is spreading, and that's just a start—everyone wants out now, see? That's what a lot of this is about—Cerion thinks they're staying for now, but Albodina already said they're pulling the plug and shipping out their staff. Right now, rates are exospheric, even in real currency, and that's only gonna get worse."

"I . . . I hadn't heard about any of that. Nobody's said anything to me about it."

"It's been all over the news! Keeping your head down is one thing, Gerr, but haven't you seen how things've been going these past couple weeks?"

"Honestly . . . no." Geren rested a paw on the bar, then withdrew it with a grimace, wiping it on his coveralls to try to scrape off the sticky slime. "You know how the company is about outside news sources, and I'm not much into news or politics anyway." He held up his paw to forestall what looked to be a rather spectacular outburst. "Also . . . hey, look . . . mostly I've just been focused on trying to save my relationship. Unsuccessfully, as of . . . I guess it's still today. Just before we all got fired."

Mally exhaled, then blinked, cooling down. Then winced. "Oh."

"I'm a very broken coyote, Mal. Between that and this . . ."

"Yeah." The panther thumped Geren's shoulder empathetically.

"He told me we were done . . . said his new guy insisted. Blocked my calls," Geren said, feeling a residual stab of hurt. "Called me selfish for not being happy for him."

"Ugh. That's rough, man." Mally's nose wrinkled up, exposing his big teeth. "You know, I never liked that guy. Can't say you're better off without him, 'cause he's got money, but—"

"Eh," Geren interrupted, trying to make the sound as final as possible, hoping to avoid further talk about Alain.

He turned away, watching a cockroach circle aimlessly beneath the rotted paneling on the far wall before scuttling back into the shadows.

"Look, I get that you're glum about all that touchy-feely stuff, but this ain't the place to mope, bud," Mally began again. "Not without help. It's life and death."

"So why are you still here?" Geren snapped, trying a more active method of changing the subject.

Mally looked away, staring down into his glass.

"I've got my reasons," he murmured after a long pause. "Can't really blab about it, but it's enough for me. But you, man . . . damn. You've been out of school what, three years now?"

"Two," Geren snapped bitterly.

"That's rough, man. You drew a couple bad ones . . . Want a drink? This one's on me."

"No." Geren could tell that Mally's 'reasons' were as much of a minefield as the subject of Alain was for him. His stomach churned. "Thanks, but no. So everyone else has left?"

Mally shook his head and sighed, knocking back the last of his drink and looking down at his paws. "Almost."

"Almost?" Geren pressed.

"Hotra and his aren't gonna make it."

"Oh no." Geren sank onto the stool beside his friend, deflating as he pictured the soft-spoken skunk with his professorial knowledge and warm wit . . . and his happy little family. "They cut Hotra, too? What happened?"

"Two hundred's as much as they'd loan him, but he needs twenty thousand more for the kid. I offered what I've got—would be a good loan for me, too, if he ever decided to pay it back. Not that money matters here, once you're outside the perimeter. Anyway, it doesn't matter anyway—even then, he's ten short. He's talking about just sending them, but Eillena shut him down, said she won't leave without him. I tried to scare her into taking it—with the truth, I might add—but you know how stubborn she is."

"Wait, wait. Hold on. Ten? Ten thousand's all he needs?" Geren sat up straight, resting his paws on the bar and staring earnestly at Mally, finally confronted with a problem he could fix. "Listen, if that's all . . . I'll give him everything I have. Get him down here right now and we'll get him his ticket."

"You sure?" Mally eyed him sidelong, mouth turned up into a strange expression. "I got something going here. I'll be ok. But you . . . and I can't take care of you or anything, even if I wanted. So don't think that. It's rough here, Gerr. It's not what you think. There isn't even a . . . thin layer of civilization to hide what it's like here. Especially once you get off of this street."

"I've got nothing, Mal." The world felt strange to Geren, but at least this one thing felt right. "That ten thousand . . . I've got nothing left that ten thousand worthless istaks can solve. If there's any hope, I can't see it. I honestly . . . I think it's the end for me. If I don't do this, my money will just go to another week in this stupid hotel."

"You may be right, Gerr. I'm not gonna lie. It may be the end soon for all of us down here." Mally looked away for a moment, biting his lip, then turned back. "You know, he may not take it."

"He'll take it. I'll tell him I've got plenty. He'll believe. He'll want to believe. This isn't the kind of place to raise a family."

"Yeah," Mally's ears were back, and he turned to stare down into his empty glass. "You're right. He'll do it for his kid. And it's good—I'm really worried for them if they stay. You're a good kid for doing this, Gerr. But you don't know much about this world out here, do you?"

"Nothing. Just that it's a subsistence society, and there's lots of crime."

"Oh man, not even." Mally raised his glass to the bartender, who nodded back and went to retrieve a bottle from the shelf. "It's hell. And look, like I said, the whole thing is at a tipping point—there's a lot of tension. You can feel it running beneath the surface. It's not a safe place to be not a local, and we're . . . ah. Look, I have a feeling it's going to get a lot worse. Let's just call it a strong feeling."

Geren narrowed his eyes slightly. "What do—"

"A *strong* feeling," Mally cut him off abruptly, making a little negating gesture with his paw, eyes flicking towards the bartender. "We'll leave it at that. But listen, if you're sure about Hotra, then I'll go get him down right now. And we . . . I . . . maybe I'll be able to help you out a little, if I can . . . where I can. If you'll let me. I know some people here, and believe me, there are some really good ones . . . though some of those don't even know it yet."

"Right." Geren felt slightly sick, but had no inclination to back out. "That's usually how it is, right? Get Hotra."

A few minutes later, a disheveled skunk was wiping the sleep from his eyes and squinting up at Geren and Mally, the emotion in his face tinged with disbelief, as if he was unwilling to allow himself to hope.

"Really. Really? You're sure?"

"Oh yeah. I've got plenty. Been saving for years. What's ten thou?" Geren spoke airily, grinning down at his portly compatriot. "I didn't know you were in trouble, or I'd have offered sooner."

"Oh. Oh, well . . . Geren, you . . . I truly don't know what to say."

Hotra had tears in his eyes, and Geren clenched his jaw to keep his smile steady and hold back tears of his own.

"Say 'ok' and let's get your tickets bought before anything changes," Mally said, glancing sidelong at Geren and sipping the latest in his series of pink drinks. "I'm worried the price'll go up if we don't, with so many people shopping tickets."

"Yes! Yes," Hotra took a hasty step towards the ticket counter, then turned back guiltily. "I mean, thank you. But yes."

The ticket agent on duty was a friendly old deer who seemed almost as moved as Hotra by their gratitude. He seemed enthusiastic about booking the departure, as if equally happy to do his part to help the skunk family escape Fonaci.

As the buck filled out the itinerary, Hotra turned back to his former coworkers, dabbing the fur beneath his eyes with his frayed overcoat.

"I'll never forget this, you two. We'll never forget this. Please stay in touch? I won't forget your loan, either, Mal. With interest. I promise."

"Just take care of your family, my friend. Worry about my interest later." Mally tossed his chit onto the counter, thumping Hotra's back lightly.

Geren tapped the release for his, careful to hide his total balance from Hotra's sight as the skunk slid his own in.

The ticket agent swiped at his terminal, and there was a long, tense moment before he looked up.

"Well, then. This is all done, and you're all set, Mr. Hotra. Three outbound for the transfer station at 25:50 tomorrow. The reservation's under your ID, and I'll be working then, so we'll have no surprises."

"Thank you. Thank you so much. And . . . thank the two of you." Hotra extended his paws and Geren allowed himself to be gathered along with Mally into the skunk's tight, tearful embrace. "You take care of yourselves. Please take care of yourselves. I'll be looking for you when I'm back on my feet. I promise."

Early the next night, Geren followed Mally to the hotel's bar after seeing Hotra's family off.

This time, he didn't refuse the offered drink.

"Well, that went well!" Mally took the two glasses of whiskey from the bartender and passed one to him.

"It's the end of the world," Geren muttered, then drank the entire glass of whiskey in a swig. It tasted terrible to him, falling somewhere on the flavor spectrum between burnt dirt and salty brine, and it lit his throat on fire. He shuddered, esophagus working to keep it down.

"Hey now. You shouldn't treat whiskey of that quality like that!"

"The shower in my room doesn't even work. It leaks this . . . foul smelling orange liquid when I turn it on. I haven't showered since I left my dorm. All I've eaten since then is two small meat plates, and that alone has drained nearly a quarter of my remaining funds. And the second one made me sick. I have three more days paid up here, and then . . . I've got nothin'." Geren's voice sounded flat and empty even to his own ears. "And that's the proper way to treat bad whiskey, from what I've heard. I've barely made it this far, Mal—I spent two and a half years in the workforce, and I feel like I'm going to be dead within a month."

"Well, here's to that, my friend." Mally raised his glass in toast, then finished its contents in a similar fashion. "Hey, it's your life after all. Let me propose a trip to a fine establishment nearby—you can at least enjoy these last few days . . . you know, before you give up and call Lapis."

"Wait, what?" Geren tensed, edging away from his friend. "How do you know . . ."

"He called me up to check on you. He's a good fella, in his own way. From Brynton, is all. So he's a little odd, so what—I'd still suggest you consider his offer. It's your best shot at survival."

"In some ways," Geren muttered, "I'm pretty sure I'd rather die."

The panther shrugged nonchalantly, but there was a glint in his eye that Geren didn't quite trust. "Suit yourself, but don't say I didn't try. That place I like ain't far away . . . maybe I can to introduce you to someone who isn't Lapis. You comin'?"

"Well . . . Yes, I suppose. Why not?"

Outside was icy and wet, and Geren's feet immediately began to sting from the cold. He shuddered, folding his arms across his chest and soldiering on behind the indefatigable Mally, who led him through increasingly seedy avenues and byways filled with shadows full of eyes before arriving at last at a big steel door.

"Now listen," Mally put his paw against the frame and grinned back at Geren. "I've been known to acquire a nubulent female or two here. Two in particular, in fact. There are some who really aren't too bad, under a light coat of grime, and not all of 'em charge. If I vanish, I'll probably be gone for the night, so . . ."

"I don't care, Mal. For once in my life I just want to drink until I black out and end up face-down in a gutter."

"Well, as I said, suit yourself. A little melodramatic if you ask me, but I'll get you on my tab, so drink whatever you like. They make 'em cheap and strong here," the panther laughed. "You might go blind, but hey, then again you might not. Hell, it's safer than the water."

Geren tilted his head up at his friend, a bit surprised by his callous attitude and wondering if he was serious.

The panther replied with a cool shrug. "I mean, it's not that I don't care, but we're in the same place, you and I. Might as well die merry, right?"

Without waiting for a reply, Mally rapped on the door with his claws; after a moment, it opened, and a pair of beefy guards looked them over.

"Hey, Mal. Who's your friend?"

"Buddy from up the plant. We both got canned, and he's skint." Mally made an odd gesture with his paw. "Gonna put him on my tab and let him have a night of it before the reality of it sets in."

"Well, welcome, Mal's buddy from up the plant." The guard stuck his head out, eyes flicking down the alley in both directions before he turned back, resting a paw on Geren's shoulder and ushering him through. "Come on in and have fun."

Geren found himself trailing Mally down a long corridor, through several sets of thick acoustic curtains into a progressively darker and louder space. They exited the last set into a dark room shaking from music with a driving beat. The walls, floor and ceiling were flowing with graphics, and . . . he squinted. The room seemed to be full of people, most of them undulating somewhat in time with the infectious rhythm.

A small, blue-lit bar graced a corner of the room, and Mally grabbed Geren's arm, leading him towards it. Three steps in, Geren found himself face to face with a hollow-eyed cheetah, who stumbled into his way and gave him an earnest stare, nose-to-nose. After an awkward moment, the cheetah pointed up at the ceiling, then laughed and stumbled off again with a flick of his tail.

"What was that about?" he yelled to Mally.

"What?" Mally yelled back, stopping.

"WHAT was that about?" He moved closer to Mally's ear.

"He's just whacked out on somethin'. The bar's got other chemistry besides just ethanol. Might be a job you can do."

"No way!" Geren's shock at the unethical suggestion was dampened by his inability to pry his eyes away from the masses of rhythmically writhing people. "And what is that? Why are they doing that? Ritual?"

Mally half turned toward him, awarding him a strange look before urging him forward again. "It's just dancing. You know, for fun."

"I thought dance was a type of performance." Geren resisted Mally's tug momentarily to watch. Dozens of people moved together with the beat of the music; it appeared ad-hoc, but the common rhythm brought a strange consistency to their motion.

"More than that!" Mally barked into his ear. "You really don't know? It's a custom, old as the ancients. Makes for a nice diversion, especially on a night like this. You should try it later! You just move with the music, like they are . . . you can even imitate the others if you want. Nobody minds! Anyway, come on up, man—we need to get you lubricated!"

He had trouble looking away, but eventually succumbed to Mally's tugging. The panther dragged him through another set of heavy curtains, and the sound dropped away to a bass rumble. Turning, Geren found himself being led, predictably, up to the bar, into the aegis of the amused doberman behind the counter. The doberman nodded to Mally, and then turned a measuring squint Geren's way.

"Silver coyote for my friend here, and bring me a Rellin drive down at Rhonna's box. Take good care of him—he needs it. Cerion, laid off . . . one of the good ones. He's on my tab."

After a minute—but perceptible—hesitation, the bartender nodded and set to work with smooth, practiced motions, but Geren felt as though he was still listening.

"Gerr, this is Kruuk. He's . . . oh, hey Kruuk! I just remembered, I wanted to ask—is Merry here? I'd like to introduce my bud."

The bartender paused for a moment, half-turning as he considered his answer; Geren almost thought he saw a disapproving flicker in his eyes.

"I haven't seen her."

"Ok, ok. If you do, let me know, ok?"

"You got it." The doberman turned away, leaving Geren no further clues as to the subtext of the discussion.

"Hey, they have food?" Geren leaned close to Mally. "I'm so hungry I'm feeling a bit faint."

"Food, no. Food is the problem here, Gerr. But ethanol-based drinks? Those are easy, and they'll help you forget being hungry."

"But . . . I mean, there's food distribution, right? How is it a problem? Isn't that a basic right?"

Mally rolled his eyes, then thumped him on the back. "Listen, I'm gonna go find a friend. You're a good egg, Gerr. Get gloriously wasted."

With that, Mally spun away, back through the curtains and into the crowd, and Geren swiveled back to the bar, staring down at its polished black metal surface.

What a strange place.

At the approach of the bartender, he looked back up.

"Silver coyote for the tall tan one," the doberman spoke crisply, setting a dented silver cup in front of him, then leaned in a bit. "Looking for action tonight?"

"Action?" Geren tilted his head.

The doberman's eyes flicked to Geren's ears, and he grinned. "Are you looking to hook up? Or, ah, rent?"

"Oh. No!" Geren flushed, sliding the drink toward him and leaning back from the bar. "I mean, I hadn't really thought about it. No, I don't think so."

The doberman laughed, then reached forward to touch Geren's nose with a pawpad. "It's alright, it's alright. There are all sorts here, for all sorts of reasons. Tell you what, why don't we just get you out on the dance floor and make some friends?"

Four hours deeper into the long winter's night, thanks to the bartender's expert hand, Geren was still coherent but certainly freed from his mortal fears and restraint, flailing in time with the music while holding the paws of a cloaked red fox of similar height and build.

Mally was nowhere to be seen.

There was something enticing and intoxicating about the fox that had initially attracted him, but he couldn't place it. They'd interacted briefly, at first, dancing near each other but not touching, then moved off to other partners . . . but they were back together a set later. As the night wore on, they'd each seemed to lose the desire to mingle and mix, making increasingly smaller circles and brushing by one another regularly.

Geren dizzily wanted nothing more than the fox's proximity; the fox wasn't clean and groomed and deodorized and perfumed and perfect as Alain had been . . . but then neither was he. Pressed against one another at last, dancing and grinding, they shared scent and shared sweat as the night rolled on, each taking increasing liberties with touch and motion and exploration while moving to the music.

At long last, as if detecting Geren's waning energy, the fox took him by the shoulder and withdrew entirely from the dance floor, sweeping him over to a little booth at the bar and settling in beside him.

"Did Mally send you to me?" Geren couldn't help but ask the question he'd been wondering.

The fox blinked once, expression blank. "Who?"

"Nevermind," Geren laughed, feeling warm inside. "What's your name?"

"Lysi," the fox said in a soft, breathy voice. "You?"

"I'm Geren. I'm really enjoying meeting you," he babbled, wiping the sweat from the bridge of his muzzle with a paw. Licking his lips, he lowered his head, looking away. "I mean, I'm having the worst week of my life, but you're making it all better."

"You're intoxicated," the fox noted in his characteristically-flat tone, light accent shimmering through. "But that's ok."

Geren lifted his head; the bartender was obviously edging towards them with a sidelong stare.

Lysi noticed his gaze and looked too.

"Lysi?" The doberman seemed surprised to see him with the fox. Almost wary.

"Kruuk." Lysi spoke simply.

"Hey, so . . . ah. This one *was* with Cerion . . ." Kruuk looked . . . concerned? Geren felt his hackles rise at the bartender's expression, though he wasn't sure why.

"Not anymore," Geren growled defensively to the fox, unsure of how that would be taken. "I got laid off a few days ago. Now I'm stuck here."

The fox reached across the table and took his paw softly.

"It's true, Lysi," the doberman said, leaning in closer. "He's, uh . . ."

"It's ok, both of you." The fox squeezed Geren's paw, turning a brief half smile up to him, then looking back at the bartender. "This isn't business, Kruuk. Really."

"Really?"

There was a strange, long moment of eye contact between the two, and then the bartender shrugged and seemed to exhale in relief. "Wow. Well, all I can say is it's about time."

Lysi shook his head, one ear flat. "Can you . . . bring him another, on my tab?"

"Yes sir," Kruuk chuckled and wandered off, shaking his head with a silly grin.

"What was that about?" Geren watched the sharp-featured canine as he began to mix another drink. "Business?"

"Nothing." To Geren's eyes, Lysi seemed slightly embarrassed. "It's . . . personal."

The fox's other paw found his and squeezed, as if to erase any censure his words might have carried. Sliding into his velvety grasp, Geren felt a jolt of excitement and clutched back almost too hard; the conversation with

49

Kruuk slipped completely out of his head and suddenly the idea of speech seemed crude and vulgar.

He closed his eyes and leaned forward, touching noses very softly with the fox.

When he reopened them, he found that his drink was made and Kruuk was nowhere in sight. All he could see was Lysi's warm, honey-colored eyes, their pupils wide in the dark.

Before he'd had more than two sips, he found himself being slowly guided toward the door. The fox took his nearly-full drink from him and set it on a little shelf beside the exit, then tugged him through into the night.

They walked for several kilometers in silence, sticking to circuitous—but unpopulated—routes, until they neared the darkened shadows of tall buildings and elevated promenades which hung debased in dilapidated decay. The tips of Geren's fur had begun to freeze, but the cold didn't seem to bother him as much as before.

"Up this way," whispered the fox, guiding him around a pile of rubble that used to be the front of a building. "Can you climb?"

"I . . . I've never tried."

"That's no." The fox's yellow teeth showed from behind a fractional grin, eyes glinting in the wan city light. "Unless you're daring."

Geren sighed, looking up at the umber sky as the fox swayed in the breeze beside him. The ethanol's effects were wearing off, but residual warmth remained which helped blur the lines of his decision-making.

"I'm feeling pretty daring."

"Good." Lysi took him by the paw and studied his face for a moment, then guided him forward.

Eventually they came to a wide, crumbling structure, looming out of the dark. It was several meters thick and appeared to be solid. Peering into the gloom, Geren could see it recede into the distance, and realized that it was a segment of wall that climbed up toward the low, misty clouds.

"Climb," the fox instructed. "I'll follow."

Geren nodded, peering upward. The section he was facing appeared to have once been at an angle, and its decomposition had led to a weathered terracing. Missing chunks served as easy handholds for the ascent, and he began to use them to work his way up, with Lysi right behind. Several sections were slick with ice, and his numb paws slid a few times before he finally reached a flat spot, hugging up against the section of wall in front of him.

He nearly jumped as the fox pressed up against him from behind, sliding his paws around his waist. A warm breath on the back of his neck preceded a soft nuzzle.

"Good." Lysi's repeated; his voice was soft and breathy, and carried surprising warmth. "One more section. Use your legs more. Don't look down."

At the fox's soft touch, Geren moved obediently forward, keeping his eyes on the climb that awaited. It was less steep, but he could see it glistening with ice, and they were twenty meters high already.

Heart in his throat, he found his grip and started up. It wasn't as bad as it looked, and before long he was pulling himself atop the wall.

One glance over the edge, however, had him flattening dizzily down against the rough upper surface of the meter-wide structure, heart beating quickly in an illogical panic.

With a rustle, Lysi pulled himself up behind him.

"You're afraid of heights?" The fox's voice was warm.

"Very," Geren confessed, looking forward and trying to still his trembling paws.

"That's good. Fear is good." Lysi offered a paw.

Geren took it, and the fox lifted him to his feet, then swung around him, momentarily seeming to hang off the edge of the wall before alighting in front with a flick of his tail.

Geren's legs went weak, and a strangled little cry of fright caught in his throat, but the fox took no heed, towing him gently forward.

"I've almost died many times," Lysi murmured over his shoulder, raising his voice against a whisper of chill wind. "But I won't let you fall. Come, if you trust me."

Without a moment's pause, Geren followed. For what seemed like many kilometers they walked along the high surface, occasionally tip-toeing over crumbling sections, or hopping small gaps. For Geren, feelings of surrender to the inevitable began to pad his fears and dull their grip, and he stopped looking down, instead watching the white tailtip of he fox in front of him, every bit a will-o-wisp leading him into the black.

Where they were going? Who was this fox? Why was he following him off into the dark atop an icy structure, high in the misty air?

He was surprised to realize that he didn't care. Without the weight of his expectations, he felt as light as a feather; things he would have been terrified of before had no hold on him. He didn't care about money anymore, or success, or failure, or Alain, or the machinations of a society beyond his control. He had no safety net, but falling free meant freedom from failure; there was nobody to judge his life or death, nor anyone to be hurt by either.

Freedom and despair were inseparably intermingled, and it left him feeling strangely balanced.

Eventually the black of the city grew hazy and darker as lights became more sporadic and snow began to fall, and Lysi began to pick his way forward with greater care until their wall dead-ended into another, higher and wider than Geren could make out. Wordlessly, the fox began to edge to the left along a narrow ledge along the face of the new wall, less than half a meter wide, tail hanging out over the darkness.

For the first time, Geren balked.

"I . . . Lysi, wait . . ."

"Come," the fox murmured encouragingly. "Put your hips against the wall and keep your tail down. It's only a few meters."

Heart in his throat, Geren felt for the snow-dusted ledge with his paw, trying to find any orientation that would allow him to safely follow. A little whimper escaped him as he wobbled slightly.

"Don't look down." Lysi offered.

Geren began to work his way out, finding the ledge wider and flatter than it had first appeared. Before long he found it widening back out, and he was across, standing on a broad, flat section.

He received another firm little embrace as his reward, and then the fox led him into a broad black opening in the face of the giant wall. As they passed through into the dark, the fox swung a metal hatch shut behind them, barring it from the inside with the turn of a wheel.

Down they went, along a sloping synthetic walkway into the relentless black, until at last an arch of light came into view and they emerged into a walled oriel high above the city, shielded from the snow by a broad, stone roof.

"There are many of these," the fox murmured, walking up to the parapet and looking out into the dark. He ran his paw over the rail, then examined it, as if checking for dust. "We don't know what they were. They might have been for hydro control before they dammed the river."

Geren stared out at the sea of ruined city which stretched from the base of the wall seventy meters below. It flowed unending to a confused horizon of buildings and decay. Threads and isolated patches of street lights, twos and threes, wove like dying embers among the burnt-out husk of a dead metropolis; in the darkness, thousands of fires winked and twinkled, and their smoke hung low, veiling the vista in a soft haze.

The fox pushed away from the rail and walked to the back of the oriel, where another little arch, less than two meters high, opened into a little adjoining alcove.

Geren followed unbidden, squinting into the darkness.

Within, a large pile of stones lay in a rough circle in the center, and dried, cut sections of trees were stacked around the edges of the circular alcove. There was a strange, pungent smell that tickled Geren's nose, and his ears perked at a windy moan from above. As he stepped further into the blackness, he could see a narrow opening in the ceiling, leading to the sky an indistinct distance above.

Lysi gathered several of the tree chunks his arms, then began arranging them in a rough pyramid atop the pile while Geren looked on in puzzlement. Their placement looked to have some sort of ritual significance, but he couldn't really make sense of it. Unconcerned with his scrutiny, the fox continued arranging things, next stuffing the area underneath the pyramid with detritus from a pile off to the side.

"What are you doing?" Geren murmured, unable to contain his curiosity any longer.

Lysi looked back at him with a slightly startled expression, holding a box he'd pulled from beneath his cloak. After a moment's pause, he shook the box over his handiwork, then fiddled with it until it clicked.

"Making a fire. For warmth." Lysi flicked his wrist and a little bright sphere appeared between two forks on the device. "You've never made a fire?"

"Never." Geren squinted at the bright light, watching in fascination as Lysi gently touched it to the center of the pile.

Moments later, a warm orange glow began to light the room, and he stared in amazement as uncontained flame began to spread beneath and rise up around the wood.

He edged back warily, unsure of how widely the flame would travel.

"Is this . . . safe?"

Seemingly unconcerned, Lysi ignored his question and stepped around the fire, gathering more of the cut trees to encircle the base of the pyramid. When he'd completed his strange, burning structure—Geren was relieved to note that the flame didn't seem to go much further than the dimensions of the stack—the fox began arranging the stones carefully around it, placing them atop one another in a little semicircle.

After contemplating his work for a moment, and apparently deciding it was good enough, Lysi slid right up against him as he'd done in the club and eased him back up into the oriel. The fox had a distinct new smell from the byproducts of the combustion he'd induced in the wood. Geren recognized it as a component of the fox's scent from earlier, but he didn't find it unpleasant.

"C'mon. It'll be warm here later."

"Is it safe?" Geren repeated. "I mean . . . will the fire spread to the other wood?"

"It's safe." Lysi's eyes glinted. He turned and beckoned gently for Geren to follow.

They returned to the overlook, where the temperature seemed to be dropping rapidly, and both leaned out to watch the night, hips and shoulders touching lightly. For an indeterminate amount of time they stood in silence, broken only by the whistle of wind and the crackling of the fire in the little alcove behind them, but eventually questions began to seep forth.

In simple conversations of few words, they talked.

For a very long time, Geren found himself saying much more than Lysi, talking and talking until his entire story was told and he had little left to say. The fox was far more taciturn, but very warm. Each word from him, when he began to speak, was worth a paragraph to Geren, who found himself enraptured by simply-told tales of survival and the history of Fonaci.

As the night wore on, the fox's tales broadened into the world around them; he painted pictures of bands of traveling traders, of people who made a living off of simply playing music for others, of secret spots and hideaways. And yet, around the fringes lay an ocean of darkness.

Things alluded to as though their existence was as normal as breathing.

Casually, in simple but bare language, the fox described street gangs, wars over housing and territory, battles over decrepit infrastructure . . . infrastructure that broke down more every day. He told stories of roving bands of predators, and the pack hunting tactics they used, and the counters to them. Little skirmishes that would break out between rival groups, and how they'd spill over into the daily lives of those around them. Stories of infrastructure that had begun to collapse decades before, and the resurgence of nature reasserting its hold on the land. Continual floods of the waterways, slides that killed people by the tens of thousands each time. Of strange plagues that would sweep through the populace with no warning, killing hundreds of thousands.

Of the death throes of a civilization.

The amount of death Lysi had seen was staggering to Geren, who was beginning to realize that his own life—despite its seeming tragedy—had indeed been quite sheltered.

"No, it's just bad here," Lysi said when Geren said so. "I didn't know my mother. My father vanished when I was young, like yours. I didn't have to watch either die. Just friends. And strangers."

Geren lowered his head, shivering at the biting chill of a sudden gust or the touch of old memories, he knew not which.

Lysi turned back to stare out across the city, and Geren hesitantly reached a paw out, resting it atop the fox's. The fox shifted his weight against him in response, warm despite the air's chill.

"I always wanted to be on a ship," Lysi's voice was barely audible, and Geren tilted his head, angling his ears to catch the fox's words. A frigid blast of air whistled through the oriel, and the fox pressed closer, gaze far away. "To work on one. You know. Go from planet to planet."

"I thought about it, too. Before dad . . . I thought about it a long time. It's why I got into engineering, originally."

"Mm." Lysi looked away. "I wish I could have. Done something like that, I mean. I always dreamed my father was captain of a ship, called away. He'd come back someday. Take me away from this place, and we'd go explore the universe together."

There was a sad innocence in the fox's voice that wrenched Geren's heart. He opened his mouth to speak, then closed it, uncertain of what to say.

"I've talked myself hoarse," Lysi murmured softly, before the silence could become awkward. "Let's go sleep where it's warm."

They spent many hours curled together in contemplative silence in the wonderfully warm alcove, touching and stroking with ephemeral softness as if each were the salve for the other's raw wounds.

Geren found that, to his wonder, he was filled from nose to tail with a sense of contentment. Even as he lay haunted by the fox's tales of ruined Fonaci—a narrative very unlike the one he'd been taught, yet with an unimpeachable ring of truth—he found himself feeling less cosmically alone.

As he drifted off to sleep under the fox's cloak and against his soft, white chest, he began to wonder if perhaps Alain had been right after all.

Hours later, Geren woke to a little shake from the fox.

He sat up, blinking himself awake. He was warm, but the wind was bitterly cold.

It was still hours before sunrise, he felt.

"We must go."

Geren rubbed his eyes, catching a glimpse of a surprisingly sophisticated-looking communications device as the fox tucked it under his cloak. He felt his ears perk, betraying his curiosity, but the fox didn't seem to notice.

Watching his night's companion pulling the frayed garment over his bony shoulders, thin frame silhouetted by the glow of the dying fire, Geren felt his emotions stir, freeing his tongue momentarily from its nervous reluctance.

"Lysi . . ." he rolled over and sat up, hesitant.

"Yes?" The fox turned quickly, eyes glimmering with an unreadable hunger.

Geren balked at the fox's sudden intense attention; losing his nerve, he turned away and buried what he'd wanted to say. "This was . . . this was nice. Thank you."

"Thank *you*," the fox settled his satchel over his shoulder and knelt near Geren. "This was a wonderful night. What now?"

Geren sucked in a little breath, paralyzed by uncertainty. "I . . . guess I should be getting back to my hotel."

The fox's expression seemed to falter for the briefest moment, then he rose, turning away. "Of course."

Geren clenched his jaw. Had that been disappointment in Lysi's eyes, or had he imagined it? He didn't *want* to go back to the hotel—he wanted to stay with the fox, at least for a while longer. Did the fox think he was rejecting him?

He took a breath . . . then let it out. His perennial fear of being rejected, himself, held an icy grip on his throat as the fox moved away, beckoning him to follow.

Out they went together without another word. Everything was colder and slicker, now heavily iced over, and Lysi led him on a different route, turning the other way outside of the metal hatch. They crossed a broad, fenced causeway and entered another little doorway in the great wall.

Gesturing for Geren to be quiet, palm down, Lysi crept up to the entrance, listening for a full five minutes before beckoning him forward. Inside was an access ladder, and he followed the fox down it all the way to the ground.

"Hey," he started, amused about being led around the long, dangerous way the previous night. "What—"

"Hush," Lysi spoke quickly and quietly, crouching down. "Come this way."

Startled, Geren closed his mouth and lowered himself. As quietly as he could manage, he followed the fox down a long set of stairs into a long-abandoned transit stop, then down to the lift path and along the tunnel. They moved in silence for a long time; Geren's legs hurt from the low, deliberate motion, but from the fox's manner he gathered that there was some unknowable danger should they be detected, and so he said nothing.

At another junction, the fox paused again, listening. Not liking what he heard, apparently, he doubled back, and they climbed an access ladder that led to the surface.

Tugging him into the deepest shadows of an alley beside a fenced warehouse, the fox nosed up to speak directly into his ear; the brush of whiskers against his sensitive flesh sent a little thrill down his spine.

"I must go. Go right, follow this street for four blocks. Stay out of sight. Four blocks. You'll come to a big street— that's Jinrong. Cross to the far side, then turn right. You're mostly safe on that street, but keep moving. Five hundred meters to Old Street. Left on Old, and another kilometer to the Niyoz. Once again—four blocks, far side of Jinrong, turn right, left on Old, a kilometer to the Niyoz."

Lysi whirled away.

"Wait!" Geren hissed.

The fox looked back with the same intent stare as before, eyes sharp, ears perked.

"Will I see you again?" Geren whispered, heart in his throat, feeling an abrupt return of the wrenching sense of loss that had pervaded his existence the week before.

"Maybe," the fox whispered back, ears flicking behind him.

Geren blinked, reading definite pain in the vulpine's wide eyes.

"Please," he whispered.

"Go." The fox hissed, then darted back, sliding into the shadows with a practiced ease and disappearing behind a large container.

Geren wanted to follow. More than anything, he burned with a feral drive to not let this fox go; every instinct told him to chase after Lysi . . . but he exercised his strength of will, forcing himself to stay.

For minutes he sat there, hoping, praying that he would see the fox re-emerge from the shadows, but eventually he turned to head back home.

"Hey! Stop, you!"

A paw gripped Geren's shoulder moments after he stepped through the Niyoz doorframe, swinging him around with enough force that he almost spilled onto the gritty lobby floor. He stumbled back, and gaped up in surprise at the stout stoat who was bearing down on him and drawing a baton.

"What the . . . I'm a guest!" Geren growled, raising a paw in protest. He drew out his room key and held it up. "Room 314!"

"Oh. Oh, no!" The stoat froze, mortified. He snapped his baton back into his belt, brushing his paws off on his hips.

His coat said 'SECURITY' in big white letters; a nametag over his left breast read 'Wally.'

"I'm sorry, sir! Sorry . . . You just smelled . . . the soot, and dirt . . . I didn't recognize the coveralls. I'm sorry! We've stepped up security after last night, f–for your protection."

"It's ok . . . it's alright." Geren blinked. "Wait. Uh . . . What happened last night?"

The stoat shifted his eyes away and stiffened, closing up instantly. "Nothing. Sir."

Geren stared at the stoat for a moment, and the stoat stared back.

"Fine," Geren growled impotently. "Is the bar open yet?"

"Not for another few hours."

"Is there anywhere I can get something to eat?"

"Well, the hotel restaurant—"

"Other than that."

The stoat looked sympathetic and thoughtful. "Beg your pardon," he started after a bit. "I don't think so, sorry to say, sir. There's a dispensary half a klick from here, but it's run by—ah, well, you don't want to go there. There's a community hydrofarm near Gechin Park that might— *might*—take istaks, but it isn't open this week."

Geren's stomach sqlched in protest, and frustration made him want to vent a complaint.

He sighed, rubbing his face. Yelling at poor Wally, if that was indeed his name, wouldn't make life better for either party . . . and it certainly wouldn't help his hunger.

He just shook his head and turned away, lifting a paw in dismissal and trudging toward his room. He was tired and sore, depressed from the wounds reopened by the fox's touch, but mostly he ached from his failure to speak up.

Lysi's abrupt departure had left him feeling very hollow indeed.

He was also starving. In two days he would be homeless. And yet the deepest pain was that he was alone again, and he wasn't sure if he'd ever be able to find the fox . . . or if the fox would want him to.

As he made his way down the corridor that led to the lifts, he considered returning to the club Mally had brought him to. The bartender had seemed to know Lysi—perhaps he could find a way to put him in touch.

If not, Geren resolved to climb to the alcove in which they'd spent the night . . . his last night not alone . . . and remain there in hopes that the fox would return.

As he exited the lift, he immediately noticed that the corridor leading to his room was strewn with debris; as he meandered down the hall, he found that most of the room doors were broken and ajar.

The door to room #314 was hanging from its hingeplates.

He didn't really care.

All of his belongings were missing, even the datastore containing his severance documents and the sack he'd carried things in.

He really didn't care about that, either.

He kicked the door shut and flopped onto his mattress.

When he woke and trundled downstairs, Mally wasn't at the bar. The barkeeper wasn't present, either; all the liquor was locked away, and the autobar was activated, flashing its selections in gooey succession.

With nothing else to do—and figuring the panther would come around sooner or later—he settled in, wrinkling his nose at the poisonous miasma of stale alcohol and funk, and saddled up to the bar's sticky, stained terminal screen.

Looking around, he found a towelette dispenser and a water tap. His attempts to clean the terminal, however, were less than successful. After a few minutes, he gave up and tossed the disgusting towelette to the side, then scanned himself in.

The terminal had his authentication data, but no other network access; the only thing active on it was a suite of time-waster games.

He debated ordering a drink from the autobar, but after looking over its filthy dispensers he decided against it.

With a sigh, he settled back in to his terminal and opened up a game to occupy his time.

He was starving.

Late in the evening, his game was interrupted by the automated announcement that the bar area was closing for the night.

Restless and tired, he returned to his cold bed.

THIRD

"MALLY?" THE BARTENDER LEANED ACROSS THE BAR when Geren approached him the next morning. The tired-looking rat planted a paw on the bar, heedless of its stickiness, peering off into space.

"Huh. Na, he hasn't been here for a few days. Figure maybe he's back to his work shift?"

"Work shift?" Geren shook his head, narrowing his eyes at the rat. "No. We all got canned. Him, too."

"Oh. That's not good, then."

"He took me to a club nearby, two days ago I—"

The bartender sucked in a breath and drew back, and Geren perked his ears, leaning across the bar.

"Do you know—"

"No!" The bartender cut him off, raising a paw in warning. His eyes flicked to the door.

"But—"

"There's no clubs in the exclusion zone. Any sort of gathering here would be illegal." The bartender turned his head away, resting a finger alongside his muzzle in an odd gesture. "So don't go nosing around anywhere for answers," he subvocalized, undertone so faint that Geren had to perk his ears to make out his words. "Especially don't go looking between

Jinrong and Xueyuan streets, around where fourth crosses."

Geren regarded the rat uneasily.

"Kid, when people go missing here . . ." the bartender muttered, then stopped, then shrugged. "Eh."

"What were you going to say?" Geren pushed.

"When people go missing here, those as go after them generally do, too." The bartender folded his arms across his chest and stared down at him. "That's all."

"Thanks for that," Geren snapped, then shoved himself back from the bar, running claws through his unkempt, greasy, tangled hair. "I don't have anywhere else to go, anyway. This is my last day here."

"Good luck with that, friend," the bartender regarded him from beneath bushy brows. "I do mean it, honest. My best advice? Stay in the grey. Least here there's a chance. Call in any favor, take any chance, any debt. Don't chase about after your friends, not if you value your skin."

Geren nodded, and spun for the entrance without another word. Unsure of whether he was looking for Mally, Lysi, or something darker, he headed straight out to the street level exit, abandoning the remains of his possessions.

His vision of the future no longer even held the casual, pyrrhic-romantic descent into animalism and death that he'd envisioned; a grey myopia had taken hold, and he had no idea what was coming next, but he wanted to find any friendly face.

Surely that was a sign he wanted to survive.

Everything around him was a grey blur as he shuffled toward the hotel entrance.

"Hey . . ."

Geren turned at the soft word, looking up.

The guard who'd accosted him was approaching, paws clutched in front of his belly,

"Sorry about yesterday, sir." The stoat wore a strange, sad expression. "You're checking out?"

Geren nodded. "It's ok. And yeah, if I come back in now, you'll be right."

"I wish it wasn't this way. Everything's falling apart." The guard hung his head. "It's a cold day, and a colder night. Did you ever get anything to eat?"

"No," Geren grimaced, unhappy at being reminded about food.

The stoat dug around in a pocket, emerging with a small, dense looking brick. Almost hesitantly, he held it out.

Geren took it, and turned it over. It was a small ration biscuit, sealed in a vacuum wrapper.

"It's only a half day's worth. Sorry."

"Thank you," Geren allowed his tone to rise in gratitude and surprise, along with his eyebrows. He tilted his head up at the stoat in an implicit question.

"We get paid in rations, here . . . Wish I had more, but it's all I can spare." The stoat half turned, looking through the door, then turned back. "Stay away from the barrels. You'll wake up to a cut throat. I'm sorry for my city . . . my planet. My people. All of this."

The clear guilt and shame in the stoat's eyes was more than Geren could bear. He looked down at his bare feet.

"Thank you, Wally. It's not your fault. I . . . I think it's ours."

"Stay safe," the stoat murmured after an uncomfortable pause, then turned away again and shuffled off.

"I'll try," Geren whispered to himself, then stepped outside.

It was sleeting.

The city, seen under the light of day, was far worse than it had seemed in the dark. Away from Lysi's carefully-relayed route, row after row of three- and four-story buildings lined debris- and refuse-strewn streets, while dead and abandoned skyscrapers hovered in the distance, vanishing into the haze.

Hundreds of gaunt, broken, diseased people hunkered in silent groups around smoking barrels full of smouldering trash; collectively, the smoke rose to form a thick haze that underlaid the yellowed overcast.

Nearly every first or second-floor window or door was broken or missing, though many were covered by rotting lumber or random pieces of synthetic prefab. In some buildings, people were encamped in the dark of the ground floor, and smoke seeped from the openings in the floors above, staining long black runnels along the outside walls.

Indeed, Geren was shocked at how many buildings were burnt out or razed entirely.

No vehicles operated in the streets; what transits there were were mere skeletons, stripped of anything of value, bones left to bleach in the sun decades before. Some were repurposed into makeshift shelters from whose shadows wary eyes glinted his way. The street lamps were largely broken, and many had been pulled down outright; signs and information displays were adapted wholesale to live new lives as lean-tos and hovels. Blood and waste spattered the once-white walks and ways, and the few trees that still grew were withered and wizened, many stripped of leaf and limb.

And this is the grey . . .

Geren shuddered.

Turning down Xueyuan Street, at last, he immediately felt himself under the scrutiny of a large group of locals hovering around a barrel. They were less-scrawny than most, and he took that instinctively as a bad sign; looking down at his feet, he shuffled by, hoping not to antagonize them. Their eyes followed him as he walked by, but nobody rose.

The third alley he checked between the two streets turned out to be the one Mally had taken him to; it looked different in the light, but he recognized the strange marking upon the door, right above the sign of a skull. The area around it was surprisingly clear, a little oasis in a world of destruction and disorder.

He had no idea what he'd tell anyone who answered, but he rapped on the door and waited.

A thin scream sounded in the distance, then twisted into a shriek and was abruptly cut off.

He hunkered down for a few minutes as his hackles and heartbeat slowly settled back down, ears a-swivel searching as he categorized the noises around him. With no immediate threat apparent, he drew a breath and stepped forward to bang on the door more forcefully.

The misanthropic grok of a spectating raven was the only thing to break the ensuing silence.

Geren banged again, then kicked a few times with the ball of his foot, but nobody came.

The wind shifted the light whisper of rain to a momentary sheeting rustle; the icy drizzle pattered down around him, semisolid.

With a soft sigh, he sank down in the freezing wet, looking around. A sheet of metal was leaned against the wall of the building, and a crate beside it formed a wind barrier. Some unidentifiable cloth had been shredded to make a bed, and a heavy plastic sack appeared to be a rudimentary blanket.

Sniffing around, he determined that the occupant of the little lean-to hadn't been around for a while, and so he decided to take advantage of the protection it offered, settling himself under it to wait.

He curled against the crate and took out the ration biscuit he'd been given, nibbling slowly with the intent of stretching it out as long as possible despite his ravenous hunger.

The long Fonaci day went by, then the afternoon, then the evening. The mist of light rain stopped for a while, then resumed, then once again became sleet, then snow grains which rustled down silently to whiten the grey.

He pulled himself close against a pile of leaves and wrapped his little sack up over his chest.

As a pup, he'd loved using his imagination; being stranded or stuck had been a fun thing to pretend, and he'd always managed to think his way out.

Geren sighed.

When he tried to think now, there were no novel solutions, no sneaky strategies, no adventuresome escapes.

There was only this.

As the night stretched on, he eventually gave up and settled in to sleep.

Late the next morning, he woke with a start. Cold and very stiff, he uncurled from the lean-to and looked around. The precipitation had stopped, but the clouds were low and grey, heavy with moisture as they scraped over the ruined city, threatening to unleash their wrath upon its denizens.

He rubbed his paws together. He was numb and sore, and shivering softly; could he adapt to this wretched cold? With a soft shake, he hobbled to the door and banged on it a few more times.

It was locked tight, and remained so; whoever might have lurked within, he decided, was either long gone or had no interest in answering.

He might as well try to find the back exit that Lysi and he had taken, he decided. None of this seemed wise, but he couldn't think of a better idea. It seemed hard to imagine that the whole club had simply vanished overnight—perhaps someone would be on that end.

After shuffling around for a while, trying both to search and to remain inconspicuous, he found a different alley off of Xueyuan Street in the vicinity of the exit. It was on the correct side of the barricaded building, but it looked nearly impassible; rubble and riverine silt formed most of a wall between the collapsing shops and tenements.

He wasn't certain that it was the same alley they'd emerged from, but it seemed like the right place. Weaving through the rubble, he carefully worked his way around piles of debris.

Almost instantly, he knew he'd made a mistake.

The shadows shifted towards him with a scrape, and he could hear strange, ragged breathing. The red shine of eyes approached quickly.

"Stop . . ." What he'd intended as a forceful command came out, instead, as a terrified whisper.

It was too much; he spun around and bolted, ears back, and heard a scurrying far too close behind him as whoever—or whatever—had been in the alley launched into pursuit.

Emerging into the street, he found himself skittering sideways on the slick, silt-covered sidewalk, and went down to all fours for a moment; a glance behind him revealed a scrawny, cloaked wretch of an opossum with a determined grimace—and a short pole shaped into a wicked-looking spear.

Desperate and weak, Geren righted himself and stretched his long legs, bare paws sliding on gritty sidewalk surface as he careened away from his pursuer. A frustrated grunt receded behind him, and the pole skittered past his feet, brushing across an ankle and barely missing a takedown.

He had no idea where he was going, other than away, and while he seemed to be gaining ground on his ragged pursuer, he could feel himself weakening quickly. He hugged the boarded-up building to his left and, at the next cross street, turned hard left and darted around the corner.

As he rounded the building, he swung headlong into a cloaked female red fox coming the other direction.

Her green eyes widened.

He slid, but was too close to stop. He started to raise his paws to fend her off, but an elbow connected with his jaw and a paw converted his motion to a helpless forward tumble. The world spun around him, and the fox as well, until he came to rest on the sidewalk.

She had somehow converted his collision to a precise throw, and now held his head in a tight grip, knife pressed up against his throat.

His pursuer came around the corner and slid, himself, falling to his side with an audible snap and a soft gasp.

He could feel the keyed-up wariness in the wiry, muscular form against his back. With a soft grunt, and shocking strength, she dragged him back against the wall of the building.

"The hell's going on?" The fox's voice was weathered, but her accent . . .

"You're from Alaran," Geren murmured, shocked.

"Yeah," she growled, and he felt the knife bite softly into the skin of his neck. "It's a fekkin' Alari reunion. Now talk."

"I w–was just running away from that one," Geren slowly raised his paw to indicate the fallen opossum, who had curled up in an injured ball. "I'm sorry . . . please, I just came—"

"Don't care," she snapped, syllables fast and rough. "Why was he chasing you?"

"I don't know!" Geren whimpered, feeling the bite of the sharp steel against the flesh under his jaw.

She sighed, then took a deep breath, seemingly to calm herself.

"I'm gonna let go of you and take two steps back. Don't fekkin' move or I'll cut your fekk'n head off."

"Ok," Geren whispered meekly.

Slowly, the knife came away from his neck, and the fox let him down.

"Lay against the wall. Don't. Move." she repeated.

Geren nodded two tiny nods, trembling and weak.

The fox looked around, stuck her head around the corner, scanned the windows around the street, then finally paced over to his pursuer. She moved with her feet apart and her knees bent, low and wary.

"Meryka?" The opossum blinked big eyes up at her, raising a paw in entreaty.

"Dagz, you brat."

"I had to," the opossum whimpered. "He was nosing around near the back door, and—"

"Quiet." The fox named Meryka dropped her voice into a commanding tone impossible to disobey.

As Dagz shrank down, Geren sat up fractionally, ears perking with interest. The back door? Were they talking about the club? Whose side was she on?

Should he take the opportunity to make his escape, while she was outside arm's reach? He glanced down the street, then drew his feet under himself.

"HEY!" Meryka snapped instantly, spinning back around to face him square on. Her black lips were drawn back, revealing broken and stained teeth, and she pointed her long knife at him. "I told you not to move!"

"Sorry!" Geren yelped, flattening himself back against the wall. The fox stared at him vexedly for a moment, then pivoted back to the opossum, though one ear stayed turned his direction.

"Me wrist," the opossum whimpered. "I'm hurt."

"Your fault," she snapped abruptly. "What happened?"

"I was mindin' my own business, like, and he came nosing around the—came nosing around."

"And?"

"Well, I know how . . . well, you know. Anyway, I chased him away, but now you've got him, so it's good, it's good . . ."

"What exactly did he do?" Meryka's speech was clipped.

"Well, I mean, he came in, like . . ." The opossum trailed off, raising a paw entreatingly.

"That's it? 'he came in, like . . .,'" she mocked. "And you kept chasing him after he left. Why?"

"Well, don't know him, so . . ."

"Your job *ain't* to defend that alleyway. Never was." Meryka sounded aggrieved, her accent waxing into a coarse backcountry drawl that made Geren homesick. "It sure ain't to chase down and kill someone for coming in it."

"Please, Merry," the opossum rose to a supplicating crouch. "You moved it, didn't you? You moved, and didn't say. I'm starving, Merry. I just wanted some food."

"We're all starving," the fox snapped. "Go back to your damn spot, and don't even think about looking back or you'll feel my steel." She dug around in her satchel, then pulled out a ration cube, identical to Wally's; with a snort, she tossed it to the possum.

He caught it, staring at it in confusion for a moment before lifting fearful eyes back up to her.

"You're released," she snapped down to him, then rounded on Geren, ignoring the dawning horror on Dagz's gaunt face. "You!"

Geren drew back nervously; the opossum rose to his feet and scuttled off the way he'd came with only one fearful glance at Meryka.

"I—" Geren started, then raised his paws in surrender as she stalked up to him.

"What exactly were you in that alley after?" Her knife was a long, precise looking thing with two edges; she held it toward him with her left paw and guarded it with her right. "Why did you go there?"

"I'm sorry! I was . . . there was a club . . . I was looking for someone."

Her fiery green eyes narrowed, but she took a beat to raise paw and push back her cowl, revealing a tangle of unkempt black hair and nicked ears behind a claw-scarred, half-snarling muzzle. Her yellow teeth glistened behind her black lips, chipped and cracked, ferocity personified. "Who?"

"Just a fox I met," Geren all but sobbed, stress blurring his vision. "Or my coworker f-from the plant, or anybody."

Meryka exhaled, then raised a paw to wipe a bit of perspiration from her eyes, visually uncoiling the tiniest amount. "Names."

"S-sorry?" Geren's breathing had become so shallow that he had to suck in a breath after the word.

The fox flinched, glancing back over her shoulder at a noise behind her, but it was just a piece of blowing trash. Her hair whipped across her face as she turned back to him, and she shook it clear, grimacing in annoyance.

"Give me names and species," she growled, ticking her claws for emphasis.

"Oh! Lysi, the fox. Male. Mally, my coworker . . . he's a panther, male . . . ah . . . I dunno . . . I don't really know anybody else here—" he stopped, sucking in a little breath; the Niyoz bartender's ominous words sprang to mind.

He slowly sank down the wall, heart beating frantically.

"What do you mean by 'here'?" Her voice compelled his instant obedience. "Tell me everything."

"The streets . . . the streets of Fonaci. I mean, Fenna City . . . the city . . ." The words spilled forth unchecked. Forcing his eyes away from the knife, he took a breath to calm his shaking. He exhaled, then took another; was he betraying his friends? Was he going to go 'missing' now?

Heart throbbing in his throat, he forced himself to continue. "I'm from the plant . . . I got f-fired . . . well, laid off . . . I mean, we all were. Not everyone who worked there, I mean, but—"

"To the point," she interrupted, but her voice was slightly softer.

"Well, so, I was at the Niyoz, but I ran out of money, and Mally took me to this club, near here, and I met Lysi and the bartender . . . I was trying to find it, but I—I—"

"Ok. Calm down, kid . . . calm down. That's all I need."

Meryka dropped her guard, and her knife flickered in the light. Geren flinched back hard enough to bang his head on the wall, but she was just flicking it dry. She wiped the residual moisture off on the inside of her cloak, then slid it behind her back.

After glancing over her shoulder again, she peered down at him a sinister expression that he realized was actually an attempt at an affable smile from a face whose humor had run dry. "Look, as long as you ain't lyin' to me, you've got nothin' to worry about from me."

With a little finger-raised gesture, she turned and scanned the street, ears a-flick, frowning at the number of people who were staring at the scene. Many stared out from behind various pieces of cover, some were passing by and pretending not to look, and others . . . seemed closer than they had been, like circling vultures.

She offered him a paw, and he took it, noting her scarred, muscled forearms where the cloak fell away from them.

"Come along," she ordered, tugging him to his feet. "It'll be ok. I'll let you go, safe and sound. Might even be able to help a bit—but if you're from the factory, I need some information you've got."

She didn't lead him back into the alley where he'd been, as he'd suspected she would, nor into a different alley to slit his throat, as he'd feared she might, but instead steered him along Jinrong Street, deeper towards the city center, moving from alley to alley. Every step found him further from 'civilization' than he'd ever been.

Eventually they came to a block of modestly tall office buildings, amidst which there were several still in operation; the signs and armed guards outside labeled them as the headquarters of the planetary government. Simple razorwire-topped fences surrounded the perimeter, and ground vehicles passed through gate checkpoints with some frequency. Communications antennas dotted the roofs.

"Stop staring!" Meryka hissed. "Look down at your feet."

Geren realized that he had indeed been staring; indeed, a guard was returning his gaze suspiciously even now. Hastily he snapped his gaze down to her heels as she tugged him along.

No alarm was raised.

After a block of surprisingly-alive—if shady-looking—businesses, they passed fifth street, and government and industry gave way to rings of flat, dingy grey six-story tenement buildings, clearly occupied and maintained.

He was just wondering if the Niyoz had been situated in a particularly bad pocket when Jinrong turned and he looked around the last tenement building and saw the sixth-street barricade . . . and the dead buildings that comprised the Fenna skyline, some crumbling away even in silhouette.

He also saw the giant wall, Lysi's wall, several kilometers away in the opposite direction, hulking over the landscape as it curved through the outskirts of civilization and wended its way toward the hills, oriels pocking its face as it turned to overlook the sprawl.

Tears sprung to his eyes as he scanned its breadth; did Lysi wait, even now, in his oriel, hoping he'd come back?

With a little sigh, he tore his gaze away. No. The odds of him seeing the fox again were low. He glanced up, then skidded to a halt as he realized that she was leading him past the barricade with its posted warning signs.

She paused and turned back to him, studying his face, her eyes shrewd.

"Nothin' for you in there," she growled at last. "Not anymore. C'mon."

He lowered his head, then sighed. It felt as though he was slipping down a hole into nowhere, and rapidly building momentum.

He followed.

Somewhat to his surprise, immediately outside"the grey" the conditions seemed to improve somewhat; the buildings were scarcely better, but there was less detritus and no people. As the street receded into mist towards city center, however, he could see the decay begin again, and sparks of fires threw their orange glow into the air.

"What—?"

"Shut up!" Meryka snapped. She dragged him towards a break between buildings.

To his surprise, there were two people sitting at a little gate just inside the narrow alley, armed with—Geren did a double take. They both held what appeared to be short projectile rifles. Despite their casual posture, they were clearly guarding something.

"Hey Merry," one of the cloaked figures said, raising a paw; the other stood and unlatched the gate.

"Hey Pizz," she gruffed. "Anyone come this way today?"

"Nah." The speaker—a silver-furred feline—pushed back his cowl. "Two of the bravos went into town an hour ago, but otherwise just local traffic since last night."

"Right. Do you have a perimeter up?"

"Negative." The guard's eyes widened. "Do you—"

"Have one up by sunset," Meryka's voice had a ring to it.

"Yes ma'am." Both guards nodded, and Meryka nodded back, adding a tiny salute-wave.

Ushering Geren through ahead of her, she closed the gate behind and nudged him on.

"Sorry to shush you," she muttered. "That corridor's like a bit of a demilitarized zone. Probably shoulda taken you round, but I don't know where my brain is today. Don't want to give 'em more info than they can get themselves, though."

"Got it," Geren replied worriedly.

Out of the alley, she led him over an odd little wall that turned out to conceal a dry culvert, which she followed for nearly a kilometer toward the heart of the city. The silence around was broken infrequently by voices and occasional hammering, but otherwise mostly remained intact save the rustle of wind and the jangles it induced.

She led him through a broad pipe, then up an embankment into the back of a warehouse. It was cleaner and more well-kept than anywhere he'd seen outside of the Niyoz, and appeared to have intact walls and doors.

There were a set of chairs around a blackened pit, and she pointed at one, setting herself across.

"What's your name?" She asked as he took a seat, voice still crisp but at her gentlest yet.

"I'm Geren."

"Meryka, but then you got that already. So, Geren, most people who are dumped from the plant leave on the first ship out. You didn't. Why? How'd you get here? Why haven't you left? Tell me your whole story."

Geren took a breath, then paused. Her style seemed too direct to be dishonest, he decided, and he had nothing in his history that really mattered to anyone . . . and so he just started at the beginning, telling her of his childhood, his parents' deaths, his years of study, his job offers and his decision to go off-planet.

She nodded understandingly at his desire to leave, again at his homesickness, winced appropriately as he described his relationship with Alain, and perked attentively as he described the Niyoz and his time at the club. He hesitated, and described his night with Lysi only in the broadest of brushes, but her expression didn't change.

When he'd finished, she flicked a paw dismissively.

"Alright," she sat up, then withdrew a datapad from her satchel. It looked similar to the one Lysi had concealed. "I'm gonna ask you a few questions about your factory. I won't answer any, so don't ask. Might be able to find you a safe-ish place to sleep tonight as trade, though, if I think you're telling me the truth."

Geren blinked. "Why the factory? What do you want to know?"

She regarded him blandly.

"Right, sorry," he muttered.

"Start with, the factory comms system ... you recall what platform it runs on?"

"Oh ... that?" Geren shook his head—that wasn't what he'd expected to be asked about. "But why ... ah, right. The comm system ... it's just the standard. Kinda old, but ... what's it called ... tri-net? Yeah, tri-net."

"That checks," she tapped her notepad, then looked up. "Did it require chip login, or did it have alternate login methods?"

"Err, it had a couple, like if your chip was malfunctioning ... it had imaging auth, pin+print, keycard ... basic auth ..."

Meryka tilted her head forward in surprise, staring at him. "Really? Basic and keycard auth? With the keycard, did you need a pin or anything else?"

"No, just the keycard. You authed once when it was assigned."

"Token auth. That's pretty interesting, I think."

Geren itched to ask her why she would be interested in the comms system, of all things, but held his tongue and waited for her to finish adjusting her notes.

"What was your job position?" She returned her eyes to his.

"I was a reaction control engineer, grade II. Supposed to be grade III as of a few days ago, but ..."

"Your factory fabs use reagent-screen catalytic production printers, is that correct?"

Geren leaned back and regarded her. That was considered confidential information, and from the steel in her eyes she knew it. He'd never even thought of disclosing it; professional ethics and law were some of the first classes he'd been made to take, and they were subjects he'd believed in strongly.

And yet his careful attention to professionalism had led him here.

"Just one question for you," he asked after a moment.

Her eyes narrowed into slits. "What?"

"Do you work for the company?"

Her eyes flew back open, and she drew back. "Good god, no."

"One of their competitors?"

"No," she snapped, lip curled. She looked wary and dangerous. "Who I work for isn't your concern."

"Ok, but . . . are you going to use this information to hurt them?"

"That's three questions, so far. But . . ." Her eyes twinkled. "Fine, I'll answer. No, I don't work for the company, no, not for a competitor—anyway, not in the sense that you mean—and yeah. With any luck, I hope to. As a start. That a problem?"

"In that case," Geren sat straight up and folded his paws in his lap. "No, it's not a problem. Yes. We form a complex multi-reagent lattice and then pass a catalyst screen through it to produce the engine cores."

Meryka's folded her arms cross her chest with a little grin.

"What parts cooling do you use?"

"The cooling process is a weak spot, if you're looking for one—it involves a saline rinse, and the effluent is pumped into cooling tanks on the southwest corner of the factory. Breaks all the time, probably our most labor-intensive area."

"What about waste heat? How do you dissipate it?"

"The pipes run outside and transfer to boiloff pond, where it's released to atmosphere. We had to spec that because the old heat release system ran out of capacity after fabs #6 and #7 came online."

"Outside of the building, but within the perimeter. Lovely." The fox tapped on her pad for a little longer, and then paused, as though she were reviewing her notes.

"Ah, speaking of which . . . not that I would know," Geren began, leaning back and crossing his arms, "but an effluent leak anywhere in the system would require an evacuation of three workfloors, and a complete stop to production for possibly up to two weeks. Lots of money lost."

Meryka grinned a lopsided grin, and a little more of her cocked tension melted away. "I'm starting to like you. Let's talk."

For the better part of an hour, she picked his brains on topics both obvious and surprisingly obscure, mostly focused on areas Geren would have written off as administrivia, and less on big, obvious things that would have interested him.

"Alright," he said at last, unable to contain his curiosity. "I'm sorry to be bold, but . . . why are you asking about the comms system, wastewater, administrative structure and so on? I would have thought you'd be interested in more, ah . . . things that would cause a long-term work stoppage, or . . . damage, or something."

Meryka tossed her well-used datapad back into her satchel and re-folded her arms across her chest, sucking on her lip. "I tell you what. I like you. Here's the deal: I agree to answer your questions, if you want. Answer anything you ask. Every reason behind every question, and every thought process. I'll tell you who I work for, and anything else I know. Only one condition."

Geren tilted his head. "What's that?"

"You'll never leave this room." Meryka's smile was frosty, and Geren caught his breath. She snapped her knife seemingly out of nowhere, and began trimming her claws. "That's the price of curiosity. What do you say?"

"Forget I asked," Geren replied quickly. "Sorry."

"Nah, don't be. My rules are for your protection. Not personal, just opsec. If you tease something out of me, the cost will be your life. Got it?"

"I see your point," Geren murmured, and he did. "I'll stop asking."

"That's the choice I'd make. Of course, I'd also spend six hours meta-analyzing this entire discussion. You might be that type, or you might not. I'm willing to live with that risk.

"I want you to know this, though—anything you tell anyone about any of our discussion could lead to deaths, and some of them could be people who are important to you. And if there is any leak of opsec on any of this, I will find you. I'm real good at that. And the price will be paid in full."

"Right." Geren felt his paws shaking softly.

He'd never met anyone in his life who scared him as much as this fox.

"Ok, I'm glad we're clear. Listen, you. I'm really lucky I ran into you—or vice versa. But I've abused your goodwill and safety enough. Now it's time for my end of the deal."

Geren shrugged warily, trying not to let himself get excited. "A place to sleep, you said?"

"Mhm. I may be able to do better, but I can at least do that. One last thing, though—do NOT tell anyone about me, got it? You might have been seen with me, I might have been seen with you and Dagz, but if anyone presses, I dragged you into an alley and knocked you out. You don't know my name or remember my face."

"Yes ma'am."

"Well . . ." She paused, then smirked. "Lysi's ok. You can tell him whatever, but only if he asks."

Geren shot sat straight up in his chair, ears erect. "You know Lysi?"

She snort-laughed, then leaned over and patted his knee.

"Nope. Sounds like a trustworthy name, though. Anyway, I'm outta time, if I'm gonna get you somewhere. C'mon."

After another kilometer walk in the light drizzle, Meryka sat him outside a nondescript door in a little cul-de-sac just as the last shades of twilight were beginning to leave the sky.

"Here's safe," she said. "As safe as anywhere. More than most—my word on it. Just . . . stay right around here, and don't wander."

"Am I guarding it, like Dagz?"

Meryka blinked, then chuckled softly. "You're funny. Sure! Have a ration biscuit."

She tossed him a cube, then raised a paw in a little salute.

"Try to stay alive, ok?"

"I'll try," Geren agreed.

She flashed him the smallest of grins, then turned away and snuck off. Free of the burden of dragging him along, she moved with a sinewy fluidity, dipping into the shadows; he lost sight of her before she'd even turned the corner fifty meters away.

He sighed; alone once more.

The cul-de-sac in which she'd left him wasn't clean, but it was absolutely empty; there were no other people anywhere around. All the doors were boarded or welded shut; all the windows were black.

"Ah well," he murmured. "Hotel nowhere."

With a little grimace, he sank down onto the cold pavement and leaned back against the wall, then turned the ration biscuit over in his hands to examine it. It was plain and beige, wrapped in a simple two-phase wrapper.

The biscuit was stamped 'RaxCo 2u universal.'

He snorted. Food distribution, indeed. He peeled back the wrapper, watching it disintegrate and lose cohesion as it encountered atmosphere.

Though he tried to savor it, the biscuit was gone much too quickly. Still, for the first time within the week he found his hunger stifled to a light rumble.

He wrapped his paws around his knees, laying his chin on them.

He was now truly alone, and doubted he'd ever see Lysi, Mally, or any familiar face again. What Meryka might have known about any of them, she'd taken with her without comment when she'd left, and he supposed he should consider himself lucky to be alive.

Like the other locals here, however, life now seemed to exist only to mark the passage of time.

An hour after dark, it began to rain and sleet once more, forcing him to unzip his coveralls and slide his head into the upper part of the over-large garment, curling up to try and stay as dry and warm as he could.

Without the light of the long day, the temperature began to fall precipitously; a cold wind channeled through the buildings, whistling and roaring into the cul-de-sac, fortunately dissipating to merely the occasional icy gust by the time it reached the street level.

Still, the cold was powerful. Sleet turned to snow, then back to sleet, pounding down around him in a steady, heavy drizzle. Every type of precipitation he knew—and some he'd never seen before—was represented as the cold set in with a vengeance. Bracing himself against it, he felt shivering begin to take hold, and the strange little feeling of optimism he'd held in Meryka's presence began to fade.

Why had he started to feel hope in the first place?

Long after dark had fallen, long before the dawn, Geren roused from a surprisingly deep sleep, awakened by the force of his own shivering.

His fur was frozen stiff, and his coveralls crinkled with ice.

With a long, miserable groan, he curled up as tightly as he could, wrapping his tail around and over his legs like he'd seen people do in holofiction and breathing into his paws. Despite his fur, he couldn't seem to get warm; his nose and throat burned from cold.

This wasn't going to work.

In the morning, he'd try to find something with a bit more shelter . . . maybe try to find his way back to Lysi's wall, though he felt well and truly lost by now.

"Hey. You alive?"

The sharp male voice was neither Lysi's nor Mally's, so he didn't care who it belonged to. He had nothing for anyone to steal. He curled up tightly and kept his eyes shut, feeling surprisingly warm.

Paws gripped his shoulders and gave him a firm shake.

"Pal, you need to move along. We can't have you sleeping out here."

Geren groaned, and received another shake.

"Hey, buddy." There was a little pause. "You're pretty cold. There's a couple of nice people with a fire going a few streets over. I know 'em, they're ok. C'mon, get up. I'll take you over there. Can't have you dying on me."

The voice had a kindly, apologetic lilt to it. It seemed almost familiar, somehow. He raised his head, rolling onto his back. It was hard to open his eyes, and his vision was blurry.

"*Geren?*" The baritone voice rose in shock.

Geren's couldn't straighten any further—his limbs were numb and he couldn't unclench his paws. He wanted nothing more than to go back to sleep.

"Geren! Can you hear me?" The voice sounded far more energetic and concerned than it should, almost panicked.

"Rrh?" he murmured in reply. The light of dawn was gently touching the sky, but he couldn't make out the blurry face in front of him . . . just a set of pointed, canine ears.

"Oh man . . . oh man . . . oh gods . . . that's what she meant! Oh gods, he'll kill me," the canid wailed. "He's literally going to kill me. *Geren!*"

Geren felt paws touching around his waist, then he was lifted up by his underarms. He sniffed; what little he could smell was distinctly canine.

Familiarity dawned, then recognition.

"'Szat . . . Kruuk?" he muttered through a stiff jaw.

"Oh thank . . . you're not totally gone. Yeah, it's Kruuk. How in the name of . . . how did you get here? Stay with me . . . we're gonna get you warmed up. Hang in there, buddy. Don't give up."

Geren nodded, then closed his eyes again, feeling deliriously tired.

After being carried for a while, then feeling his legs thumping down a set of stairs and dragging down a hallway, he was stretched out on a flat surface. He felt . . . very strange. Warm, but numb; analytical but incoherent. His eyes could make out blurry shapes, but it was hard to focus his mind on them—or anything else.

Heavy bootfalls receded rapidly, then a door slammed shut nearby and he was alone. Still, he could feel warmth around him, and that gave him a bit of hope. After a few minutes, there was a click, and the boots came back, presumably with their owner.

"Yeah?" It was Kruuk, but it sounded as though he was speaking to someone else. "Yeah. Extremities are at about sixteen. Core is . . . yeah. Yeah, it is. Yeah? Hold on."

Something prodded softly at his nose, then bumped against his numb paw. He could feel things wrapped around his paws and arms and neck and legs, and something warm and wet was placed over his face and eyes. His ears pricked up, making out the lightest buzz of an earpiece speaker coming from Kruuk's direction.

The words were unintelligible.

"Eighty-six percent saturating. Oh?" Kruuk sounded worried, walking away from the table. "Ok. It's all climbing. I have those here, yes. You'll come—no, no, I will definitely do that. So you'll—no. I—no. Listen, I've already scrubbed you for tonight. I'm putting Merry herself on. No. No! But they don't need to know that."

There was a long pause.

"Captain?"

There was another buzz, and Kruuk sighed. "Oh, ok. Yes. He is, yes—can you make it back tonight? No. I told you no—this isn't a rank thing. Ok. You agree, then, right? Ok, good. Good. See you then."

Kruuk sighed, then walked back to the table.

"Doing ok, bud?" Kruuk's tone was much softer, as was the gentle paw that touched his chest.

"Yes," Geren's voice was a bare hiss. "Thank you."

There was a click, and a light buzzing filled the air; warmth began to surround him, along with a slight increasing numbness and an ache that spread from his jawline down to his stomach.

"Thanks," he rasped again. He blinked crusty eyes, perking his ears and trying to sit up.

"Ah-ah. Stay down, and breathe slowly. You'll be ok here in a few hours, but for now don't move. You can sleep in here . . . it's safe. Here, lift your tongue."

Geren did as instructed, and felt something cool placed beneath it which dissolved in his mouth. A soft wrap encircled his muzzle, and suddenly every breath brought with it warmth and moisture.

Though he briefly tried to fight somnolence, he almost immediately slipped under.

When he awoke from tortured dreams a few hours later, sore and stiff, he found himself alone on a bed of straw. He pushed himself up, dislodging a thick pile of ratty blankets, then stretched lazily, wiggling his fingers and toes. His scent was stronger than usual, and his belly was rowling angrily, but aside from a slight tightness in his chest, he felt . . . somewhat more normal than he'd expected.

One old-fashioned field oximeter was clipped to his toe, and his lips were sticky; touching them with a paw, he found that they had been lightly coated in a thin oil.

"Thank you, Kruuk," he murmured softly, then sighed.

He wasn't ready for this. He'd only been saved by . . . what had he been saved by? Luck? Unexpected friends? It was at once troubling and reassuring . . . but he knew in his gut that he wouldn't last like this.

He blinked blurry, crusted eyes and looked around.

He was in a small, warm room, with metal walls and roof. Barred windows high above the well-worn wood floor allowed ingress to the fading twilight; some sort of oil-burning furnace was cobbled together in the corner near his bed, rumbling and shaking as if it were going to fall apart any minute. Buckets of water had been placed around its vents and hotspots, and the air was relatively humid.

Heaven, comparatively. It was so sybaritic that he found himself settling back down and stretching out. He'd leave when asked, but until then . . .

With a dizzy, exhausted sigh, he pulled the blankets up to his chin, closed his eyes, and slept for many more hours.

"Hey, sleepy." A familiar, tender voice intruded on a delightful dream.

Geren woke with a start and a little gasp, looking up to find a pair of tired honey-colored eyes regarding him.

"Lysi!" He pushed himself up to sit, then wiped his face with a paw.

The fox was kneeling beside him, wearing a camo-patterned grey jumpsuit and boots, with goggles pushed up to his forehead. A black projectile weapon hung in a holster strapped to his thigh, its menace an odd counterpoint to his soft expression.

"We lost track of you," Lysi murmured, brow creased in worry. Geren felt his heart flutter a little, and his mouth went dry. "I had to be sure who you were, but then your friend couldn't find you. You left the hotel?"

Geren swallowed, rising to a squat. "Mally's ok? He's alive?"

"He's fine," Lysi murmured. "Why leave?"

"I ran out of money. I only had a small amount, and I couldn't stay. I tried to find you, but didn't even know where to start. After that . . . things got strange. There was a fox—"

"Meryka," Lysi supplied.

"Yeah." Geren was relieved. "Anyway, she brought me over here, and told me it was a safe place to sleep. Then Kruuk showed up . . . you're nodding like you know all this."

"Meryka is . . . discreet. Always trust her."

"I decided to," Geren murmured, glad that he hadn't betrayed his friends. "Not that I think she would have given me a choice. She's intimidating."

"She's deadly," Lysi's voice carried an appreciative edge, and his eyes sparkled. "Kruuk was supposed to come last night, but didn't understand. Enough about . . . all this. I'm sorry we left you behind." He shifted forward, touching Geren's leg with a soft, warm paw. "I'm sorry I left you behind. I won't do that again. Promise."

Speechless, heart in his throat, Geren lifted a paw to stroke his claws through Lysi's cheekfur. The fox immediately pressed forward and rubbed his cheek against his palm, then grasped both of his paws and nosed up to brush noses with him. Geren felt dizzy as the fox's breath wafted through his muzzlefur, and his eyes drifted shut. With agonizing slowness, the fox moved forward and kissed his lips, holding it for the briefest of moments before pulling back.

Geren felt his breath escape in a sigh of pure release, and he drew back, surprised to find himself moist-eyed.

"Come home with me?" Lysi whispered, eyes wide and sincere. "It's not much, but it's mine. Will you come?"

"I'd follow you anywhere," Geren breathed.

FOURTH

MANY HOURS BEFORE THE LIGHT OF DAWN would threaten to contaminate the long Fonaci night, two forms nearly equal in height left a large storage building to meander down a filthy corridor beneath the wing of an abandoned factory.

They made their way in silence through gaggles of bedraggled folk huddled around meager trash fires, around fences long neglected and across a frozen field before arriving at an old, run-down tenement building. Entering in a hush, they tip-toed down reeking corridors until at last they came upon a simple red door.

It opened to Lysi's pawprint, and the fox ushered Geren into the darkened room, stepping through after him and closing the door behind.

Wordlessly the fox guided him through the darkness to the little metal-framed bed in the center of the tiny room, sliding out of his flattering—and incongruously fancy—jumpsuit to reveal simple, dingy undergarments and soft white underfur. The fox stepped out of his boots, kicking them to the side.

Geren opened his mouth to speak, but Lysi pressed forward in that instant, sliding his paws around Geren's waist and closing the gap. Forerunner foxwhiskers swept softly against his lips to commingle with his own; at the electrifying touch, he forgot entirely what he was going to say.

The fox opened his muzzle, his black lips parting and brushing lightly against Geren's.

Another tingle ran through Geren, nearly incapacitating. His paws trembled as they reached for the zipper on his own coveralls, but Lysi's were steadier and quicker and had the zipper down to his thighs nearly instantly. Warm, nimble foxpaws traced up to his shoulders, sliding the coveralls off and tugging them down even as the fox pressed forward into a little kiss, little yellow-stained teeth bumping with his.

Geren's desire began to steadily wash into a desperate, hungry lust, and he allowed himself to be pushed gently onto the bed, weak and overcome by need. Suddenly, nothing existed outside of Lysi; despair, desperation and confusion all melted into an effervescent desire that washed away any articulate thought or notion of restraint, and he stretched out on the lumpy, stained mattress, tugging his lover down with him.

Lust washed through him, but just enough willpower remained for him to raise his head slightly.

"Are . . . are you clean?" he whispered.

"Mm." The fox's tail swished behind him, and he tilted forward, resting his paws on either side of Geren's head and locking gazes with him. He tilted his head, ears forward; his expression was placid and calm. Geren found himself lost in wide, honey-colored eyes, framed by light, wavy hair.

"Does it matter?" the fox murmured with a soft blink. "In this city, my love, love and death are all we have."

Lysi pressed forward slightly, touching noses with him, breath washing through his whiskers and carrying away the crumbling remnants of his inhibitions.

"So?" the fox whispered, a strange little smile on his face. "Does it?"

Geren trembled beneath his foxy lover and closed his eyes, feeling tears running backwards from his eyes. The first tears he'd actually shed in years.

The first he'd been unable to hold back.

"No," he breathed. "No it doesn't, beautiful fox."

Several hours later, Geren lay half awake, tucked beneath the fox.

The room was dark, and the air was both frigid and humid, a dank, icy chill . . . but the fox was curled with him, entwined, and he felt warm to the core. He also felt dizzy and he needed to use the restroom, but he didn't want to disturb the sleeping Lysi.

The scent of the room, the events, and even those of his partner registered with every breath; they weren't exactly pleasant, in a classic sense, but he didn't care at all.

It was as if he'd fallen through a faultline, and he had little interest in what lay behind—thoughts of everything from his former life met a resounding disinterest.

He had no idea what the future would bring, but, reflecting on it, he was surprised to conclude that he felt little fear. He'd awakened from a haze of conformity and a malaise of depression he'd not realized himself to be in.

In retrospect, it seemed obvious that nothing in his life had ever gone right. Work, school, social life, youth—he'd been stymied at every turn.

Despite excellent marks from a very good school, he'd been turned down by every employer he'd sought an interview with until Cerion. Every attempt to elevate his social strata or mingle with the cliques of Alain's social class had failed, and had eventually been rejected by the one person he'd fallen for.

He blinked, looking down at the curving form of the fox nestled against him.

The one person he'd fallen for . . . before tonight.

In all the years he'd been with Alain, he'd never felt such unrestrained lust and passion. There was something about Lysi that was pure magic, and he wanted the moment to never end. It probably wasn't love on Lysi's end, and he wasn't entirely sure what his own emotions were leading him to, but he didn't care—something inside him had shifted in some tiny but profound way.

At the moment, at what should be the lowest point of his life, all he knew was that everything suddenly just somehow felt less wrong.

Nuzzling gently into the joint between the fox's neck and shoulder, he closed his eyes and sighed, trying to ignore the pressure in his bladder and regain the oblivion of sleep.

Geren woke to the touch of a paw stroking through his chestfur. Momentarily dissociated, he sat up with a start, surprised to feel a soft body against his own—a body that smelled nothing like Alain.

He found himself enveloped in a warm embrace, which he returned instinctively—if a little mechanically—before glancing down to see a swath of red-orange fur glistening in the weak light of day which shone through the broken window of the little room. His eyes widened as his memories returned, and he experienced the shortest denial/anger/depression/acceptance cycle of his life, inside the span of a breath; at its conclusion, he clutched Lysi tightly to him, burying his muzzle against the fox.

"Good morning," he murmured warmly. His sleepy languor, tinged with the mildest of headaches, was slow to fade.

"Mm," the fox whispered back. He pushed Geren back down against the bed, nosing down at his nose, his eyes bright. "Welcome to the day."

Geren grinned, which segued into a yawn, which became a stretch. When it was all over, he propped himself up on his elbows and looked around. It had grown so late in the thirty-five hour day that the sallow daylight oozing through the broken window was waning once more into the ugly orange of sunset.

Looking around the little apartment, he felt a little shudder trickle down his spine.

That anyone lived like this was somewhat of a shock to him—when he'd come to Fonaci as a new hire, the little cabin on the ship had been larger, and far more well-appointed. The stateroom on the passenger liner to Hope had been easily twice the size.

Lysi's tiny little studio had no heat, and the one window, high in the wall, small and broken, was propped open to let in fresh air. The air smelled of spice from neighboring kitchens mixed with the basic visceral smells of sweat, fox, coyote and the stale odor of others before.

Right in the middle of the room, dominating what little space was left, sat a square structural support pole, as if the room had never been designed for habitation. The faded walls were mildewy and stained with who-knew-what, and the floor was grimy and bare.

A curtained-off section in the corner appeared to serve as the bathroom.

Geren glanced back down to find the fox in his arms watching him with a pensive expression, and suddenly he didn't care at all. He sat up and wrapped his paws tightly around Lysi's chest, nuzzling into his hair, and the fox's tension faded palpably.

Nuzzling became nibbling, and his nibbling was returned.

A paw found the back of Geren's head and slowly guided his kisses and nibbles muzzle downward across the fox's neck–which he nuzzled–to his chest–which he lapgroomed–to his belly–which he sniffed–then pushed his muzzle lower.

Despite the impossible-to-ignore twinges from his swollen bladder, Geren set to his task with enthusiasm, working to elicit every squeak and drawn-out whine he could from his lovely partner.

The experience . . . Geren's mind started to compare it to his past experiences but dismissed it on the spot.

There was no comparison.

He paced himself, teasing slowly. Time itself was limitless; there was only the lovely Lysi and the end of the world. After a while, however, his concentration began to falter, and he pulled away with a little lick, leaving the responsive fox right on the edge.

"Sorry, sexy fox . . . but if I don't hit the head, I'm gonna soak your bed," Geren giggled.

"Go ahead," the fox said huskily.

Geren blinked, then grinned sheepishly.

He shifted to stand up, but Lysi's paw tightened in his hair and pulled him back down to his crotch, rising a little and tugging Geren's nose against the heavily-scented white fur. For a moment, held there, Geren was overwhelmed by passion and desire; after another moment, driven by his biological necessity, he tried to straighten again, whining softly.

He felt the fox's paw reluctantly release, stroking down across his muzzle.

"Oh fine," Lysi said, sounding amused. "Over in the corner. There's a curtain if you must."

Geren shuffled toward the indicated corner of the room, though his nose could easily have found it for him. The facilities consisted of a simple U-shaped depression in the worn synthetic flooring; as he addressed it, a physiological sense of relief washed across him.

No sooner had he finished than he found the fox's behind him, paws pulling him back to the well-used mattress.

Hours later, exhausted and spent, they lay together, sharing heat against the cold.

Eventually, the fox arched into a big stretch, then sat up, peering down at him again.

"Ever been outside before all this?" Lysi's light brogue added a musicality to his plain words, Geren decided. "Of the factory, I mean."

"No, not really."

"Hm." Lysi pushed him away, holding him at arms length and looking him over, frowning thoughtfully. Without a word, he swung out of bed and stepped over to the room's single table, a cluttered metal folding worktop, rummaging around until he'd freed a bowl covered in a cloth.

Geren felt his stomach rumble, and he licked his lips. Part of him hoped it was something edible; another part of him was worried that it would be.

It turned out to be a tub of white powder; Geren tried to sniff it, but the fox gently pushed his nose away, handing him the cloth.

"Not food," Lysi murmured, voice warm. "Lay back, and breathe only through this cloth."

Confused but obedient, Geren shifted back onto his back and draped the cloth over his muzzle; Lysi wrapped another around his own mouth and nose, then began to drizzle the powder into Geren's bellyfur.

"You came back." Lysi murmured, eyes flicking to his, then away.

The fox began working the powder into his roots, moving slowly up his chest. The touch of his paws was sensual—it wasn't possible for it not to be—but business-like as he carefully covered one section at a time. "Lift your arms."

"I . . . yes, I did. I shouldn't have let you go," Geren said, tilting his head. He raised his arms to touch the bars of the bed's endframe; the cloth started to slide away from his muzzle, but Lysi caught it quickly and pushed it back into place.

"Don't breathe this," the fox murmured, tilting his head.

"We have bad things here. Bad parasites that bring disease."

Geren trembled softly, captivated by the gentle concern in Lysi's voice. As the fox worked the powder under his arms, his muzzle brushed lightly against Geren's, and he felt himself lifting his head, eyes drifting shut.

"But you came back. For . . . me?" Lysi's voice held a strange hesitancy.

"Yes, for you. I was terrified that I'd never see you again. I couldn't bear the thought of it. I was so angry with myself for letting you get away—I almost broke down. I just . . . I felt like I was adrift in space, running out of air, and suddenly you were there."

"I had to go, before." The fox paused, looking him in the eyes. "Without you. I had to have you checked. And I didn't think you'd come back."

"You're pretty," Geren whispered, lost in his eyes.

"You're pretty," the fox countered, stroking through his fur. Geren's breath caught as he realized that the fox's eyes were just as warm and loving and moist as he felt.

"I . . . think I love you, fox." Geren whispered even more quietly, trembling. "I don't want to leave."

There was a long, awkward pause, and Lysi's expression was unreadable.

"Not safe to go above the shoulders," the fox murmured at last, then pushed him down, rubbing his chest lightly. "Roll over."

Heart racing anxiously, Geren squeezed his eyes shut and turned over onto his belly, keeping his arms up. The fox's warmth settled against his rump, and he felt more of the powder being rubbed into his back.

He wanted to bite through his lip, stress building as he kicked himself for being so forward. His nose had told him that for the fox, this was most likely a simple little tryst— one of many—and yet he himself was professing his love after only the second time they'd met.

Stupid! Stupid.

Months. It had taken months to work up the courage to ask Alain to live with him in his little dormitory, and the crushing rejection still echoed within him. Part of him still suspected that that very request was what had caused Alain to pull away.

He had no idea what had prompted him to be so forward.

Lysi's paws worked the powder into his sides and hips, and he felt the fox lean down against his back until foxwhiskers brushed his ear.

"'Sometimes the price of freedom must be stolen from one's pocket.' Dad used to say that," Lysi's breathy voice was soft. "But I never understood. Until now."

Geren twitched at the fox's gentle earnip; he exhaled in desperate relief, sinking forward into the pillows.

"Don't leave," the fox whispered. "We're just getting to know each other."

FIFTH

As soon as the sun had fully set, and the last of its amber light had left the sky, the fox retrieved his own wadded-up undergarments and a rumpled cloak from the floor and tossed them to Geren with a slight smile.

Geren donned the fox's underwear and cloak, shaking himself to settle it across his shoulders then watching as Lysi slid, in turn, into the throw-away coveralls he'd been given at the factory.

The fox's military-esque garb was nowhere to be seen, he noticed, but decided not to ask about it. In time, perhaps, the fox would choose to share his secrets.

The past few days seemed almost dream-like in his memory.

Once dressed, Lysi grabbed a light sack by the door and threw it over his shoulder.

"Come." The fox took his paw.

Lysi lead him out of the tenement building and around a large hill of trash. Down they went, threading their way between two collapsed buildings and around a caved-in pit; stepping carefully, they traversed through the ruins of a long burned-out park, then crossed a dark, rushing river, balancing on rotting planks strung together over a crumbling weir.

On the other side, another trail led through a debris-strewn field then into a little overgrown cobblestone plaza.

The wind was wild, warm and wet, tearing through the streets and rattling the metal warehouses, shaking the hovels and lean-tos that lined the district. Soft flashes lit the distant sky from time to time, and rumbles shook the ground; a fine mist of precipitation moistened the land and Geren's fur, and he licked his lips thirstily. He quickly regretted it, however—the rain water was acidic, with a strong sulfur taste, and he found himself spitting repeatedly to get it out of his mouth.

He had no idea where the fox was going, but being guided through this dangerous land was taking on a surprising normalcy for him. The magic of mutual attraction was stronger than ever, and the further he fell in to living in this fetid, filthy world the less he found himself caring where his journey brought him . . . as long as it involved Lysi.

There was just something about the fox.

For his part, the fox seemed happy to walk paw-in-paw with him, scarcely ever more than a touch away; his casual affection made for an odd contrast to the wary alertness of his ever-moving eyes and ears.

After much hurrying through narrow alleys and by-ways in a tacit bid to beat the oncoming storm—and after a brief sprint away from a sick, mange-ridden raccoon with a makeshift knife—Lysi led him past a broken-down fenceline into the ruins of a lightless office building which reached its mass high into the gloom above, making it under cover just as the first drops of rain began to patter against the desolate court before it.

Less than five meters inside the entrance, they were stopped by three cloaked figures. Lysi held his paws up and, confused, Geren followed suit.

"Who's this?" A thin, splotchy canid with odd, round ears darted around Geren, holding a rather non-makeshift knife and a scanning device. She seemed high-strung, and Geren shivered, trying to radiate calm. "You know this guy's chipped, right?"

"Yes, I do. Geren, these are my best friends," Lysi put his paws down and tugged Geren to him, almost protectively. "Maven, please. Put the knife away. Geren is from the factory. They released more of them with no way out."

Maven sniffed at Geren, then snorted. "I see, I see. I see the two of you already made good friends."

"Don't make me regret coming, Mav," Lysi said calmly. "I was excited to show him off, but I won't have him frightened or insulted."

Geren swayed, swallowing a lump in his throat.

"Oh, c'mon. I'm just kiddin' around, Lyss. You know me. Just surprising, you know, to see you bring home a stray." Maven glanced sidelong at Geren, licking her lips. "Does he speak for himself?"

"I do. At times," Geren's voice broke, and he cleared his throat. He wanted to ask where they were and what they were doing, but that seemed importune, and he bit off the question, gazing uncertainly at Maven. He felt like he knew her species, but he couldn't quite place it.

As if to introduce themselves, the other two lowered their hoods; one was a zebra with heavy facial scarring, the other a grinning silver fox with most of an ear missing. They, too, had weapons—the zebra had a machete sheathed across his chest and the fox leaned casually on a shillelagh with a metal head.

"He risk," the zebra said, his deep voice resonant, accent strange to Geren's ear. "Risk you as longs as he have a chip. Bad bring."

"He's from Alaran. They're all chipped there." Lysi's expression read, to Geren, slightly worried. "What's a little risk? Hm?"

"Risk as longs as have a chip," the zebra shook his head, voice monotone in his disapproval. "Not is problems."

"Let's go in," the silver fox stepped up, peering back through the gaping doorframe. The angle of his body tacitly prevented the Zebra from physically stopping Lysi and Geren from moving through. "Don't trust this night."

"No, there's an odd feeling about," Lysi agreed, placing his paw in the small of Geren's back and easing him forward, past any other objections that might be mounted. "Is there a boil going? I brought my rybiniums."

In the center of the office building—which, as they proceeded further, Geren could see was heavily fire-damaged—there was a lift. As they approached the door, the zebra reached out and forced its doors open. There was no car. The fox tossed his shillelagh in and Lysi bit down on the top of his jute bag, holding it in his mouth.

One after the other, they made their way down a rope ladder into the lift pit. The maintenance door at the base opened from the inside to Maven's swift triple knock, and they all filed in past a sturdy weasel cradling an old projectile carbine.

The air was smoky and dry in the enlarged room, and the odor of cooking meat and hot metal reached every corner. A wide sheet of thin steel rested across a pair of welded steel tubes, forming a rudimentary table with many chairs, not a single one like any other.

Other little mattresses and old couches sat in corners and sides, and here and there small groups knelt, sat or lay around them. Another steel slab in an alcove at the very back of the room was being used as a cook surface; what Geren had come to recognize as an organic material fire burned under it, and ducting was in place to carry the smoke to a higher floor.

The cooking food smelled amazing, and he found himself violently hungry, almost to the point of nausea.

"My friends," Lysi said softly, beaming at them. He stepped inside and lead them to an old semicircular couch with a table in the middle, ushering Geren into the middle before dropping his jute and sliding in to sit.

"What do we have?" Lysi asked, once everyone was seated.

"Spices," the zebra said. He lifted his cloak to reveal a well-muscled—but extremely thin—torso. A folded cloth hung from his belt, and he pulled it free, placing it in the center of the circle with Lysi's package. "Two pouch of zorcacums, bak bak. One capsicums."

Lysi beamed at him, paw clutching Geren's thigh happily. "Wonderful, Zori. That's wonderful! Coriagh?"

The silver fox shook his head. "I'm empty-handed. I lost my beets to a shaker a few hours ago—you'll have to carry us this time with your rybiniums, Lyss."

"Well I have a big pack of mushrooms," Maven broke in, sounding smug. "And," she looked around, then leaned forward; reaching into her haversack, she pulled out her own cloth-covered bundle. When she unwrapped it with a fatuous smirk, Geren was surprised to see five rather small, dry-looking onions presented like a treasure. "These."

"Oh!" Coriagh clapped softly, displaying his dentition in a merry, snaggletoothed grin. "Lovely."

Lysi placed each offering in its own cloth and then opened his own parcel, revealing at least a dozen withered tubers. He wrapped them all up in a bundle and wandered over to the cooking area, Coriagh in tow.

Geren watched him go, disturbed anew by the fact that it appeared that these friends were bartering for food—he had nothing to offer; would he go hungry? And why would they have to barter for food? This was a central world—subsistence was a guaranteed right. Something was very, very wrong with this planet. How could things have ever gotten this bad?

He jumped at a touch on his shoulder; when he looked up, he found the zebra's big eyes fixed on him, unblinking.

"Lysi like you, trekpak." Zori's voice was quiet but deep with warning. "I likes Lysi but not yet you."

"I . . ." Geren was uncertain what the zebra was trying to say. "Ah—"

Maven leaned close, speaking through bared teeth. "Meaning that if you screw with any of us, if you steal from us, or if you ever hurt him, in any way, we're gonna chop you to pieces. He's our friend, not you. I don't like you. I don't trust you. If you weren't his, you'd be dead already. Clear now?"

Geren drew back and sat in silence with a tiny nod, then turned to look away. Across the room, a hyena looked up at his gaze and scowled, and he flinched, lowering his eyes to the table.

After a few minutes, Lysi and Coriagh returned with two small jugs—one full of clear liquid, one full of something a vibrant red—and four mugs.

The tiniest turn of Lysi's lip hinted at his satisfaction as he deposited them on the table and slid back into place.

"Drinks, fresh water. A full serve each. And—"

"Full including him?" Maven's lips drew back in a scowl, and she indicated Geren with a thumbclaw.

"Yes," Lysi answered placidly. Only a slight lift of his eyebrow indicated his surprise.

"What did he give? What's he done for us, other than work for the thieves who steal our food?" Maven gestured at him, and Zori nodded in concordance. "I know you like him, but look at him—he's probably never been hungry a day in his life! I don't see why my effort should go to feed him."

"Then he may have mine," Lysi said in a soft, friendly tone of voice. "He's very hungry now."

"No." Geren shook his head, although his stomach was actually growling with hunger. "I don't need food, it's fine."

"Lyss' rybeniums made up most of the deal, Mav." Coriagh shifted towards Lysi, and suddenly there was a physical divide in the party.

A strained silence fell.

"I should have asked first, but I didn't think it'd be a problem." Lysi leaned forward, ears perked. "But . . . I also managed a bit extra for everybody." He pulled out four small metal discs and placed them gently on the table, whiskers flattening back as he tried to form a smile.

Geren clutched softly at Lysi, reading concern—and confusion—in the fox's features.

"That's a good bargain, Lyss," Maven murmured, subsiding a bit and stroking her chin. "Very good. I haven't managed a shower token in weeks."

"Iella. Good, yes," the zebra muttered in his basso voice, then shook his head, glowering at Geren and raising his hand. "But want for Zori, Mav, Lysi, Cory. Me and not him not contri-buted."

"Yeah," Maven hardened again. "You need to show it right how it is, right from the start."

"Look, it's ok," Geren said softly. "I'll sit this one out."

Lysi leaned over and draped a paw loosely over his shoulder as if claiming him, nosing his cheek in tacit reassurance. Geren closed his eyes and leaned back against the fox, trembling softly from the sudden stress.

"He agree, even." Zori pointed at him, puffing out his chest.

"The two of you!" Coriagh snapped, glaring down at the others. "I can't believe you. Geren has nothing and nobody, no money, nothing to trade, and nowhere to live. He nearly died already, and he's not eaten for days. And there's more than enough coming for all of us to fill our bellies—even you, Zori, who always eats most. And Lysi's rybeniums were most of the damn bargain. And this is *Lysi* that we're talking about. Do you have any idea what he does for you? How hard he works for—"

Lysi grabbed Coriagh's shoulder and he stopped, snapping his mouth shut in exasperation just as Maven rounded on him.

"You're one to talk!" Maven barked at the dark-furred fox, teeth bared. She seemed oblivious to the exchange. "Where's your contribution? Why should we listen to you? Why should you get—"

Coriagh was on his feet in an instant, shillelagh in his hand and raised. The motion was so abrupt that Maven cowered back against the zebra with a sudden gasp, and Geren shrank back against Lysi.

The neglected jugs wobbled on the table.

"Why should you? Because I put in more every time, maybe? For years? Because you don't know the half of what Lysi—"

"Cory." Lysi spoke quickly, tone carrying a note of warning. "Enough."

Maven looked angry, if a bit scared; the zebra shifted, as if ready to spring to his feet in her defense.

"Sit down," Lysi's voice was soft but firm, and he tapped the table. To Geren's surprise, after a moment of pause the objects of his command reluctantly complied. "He eats. My share."

"And as I'm apparently a freeloader as well," Coriagh's tone was biting. "I'll give my share to Lyss."

Maven growled into the ensuing silence, nose wrinkling in stubborn distaste.

"Stop this." Lysi seemed slightly annoyed, but from the light shaking of his grasp Geren knew the fox's emotions ran far deeper than he let on. "I can't believe you're behaving like this in front of my yotie. I am ashamed of you. He knows nothing of our society, or you. This is what we show?"

"We works for meal, hard works." The zebra straightened his shoulders, pushing Maven away and pushing back from the table. "Does not good to shows him bad."

"Zori's right," Maven stated, still eying Coriagh warily. "We've all worked for it. He's done nothing but be hungry. I say no—no contribution, no food. It's not personal, but no freeloading. It's a rule. The rule here, and he's gotta learn."

"I regret coming," Lysi said, voice flat. "I'm sorry for this, Geren."

Geren could think of nothing appropriate to say, so he squeezed the fox's paw. To his surprise, Lysi squeezed back and stood in one fluid motion, tugging on Geren's paw softly until he rose. The fox retrieved one disc from the table and slid it into the front pocket of his coveralls.

"We're leaving."

"Me too," Coraigh leveled an acid glare upon the other two as they both began to voice protest.

"No." Lysi lifted a restraining paw, gentle but firm. "You stay, Cory. You haven't been eating well, and I need you strong and healthy."

Coriagh and Lysi shared an oddly meaningful look, but the silver fox settled back into his seat.

"Is not for you going," Zori said plaintively, blinking his broad eyes in confused dismay. "The singings later, and storms?"

"I'll take the storm to this. Any storm. You'll just have to perform without me. Come, yotie," Lysi's voice dropped affectionately, warm and reassuring, and he tugged Geren towards the exit.

"Wait!" Maven's voice came from behind. "No, no, no . . . come back. Lysi!"

Lysi did not slow or turn; Geren tried not to clutch at his protesting stomach or trip into any of the other groups.

The guard lifted his head in slight surprise at their quick departure, but opened the door for them without a word.

"I'm sorry. Please come back!" Maven's voice rose lightly across the room.

Lysi stepped through into the dark shaft, and Geren followed.

At street level once again, Lysi didn't make for the exit, as Geren thought he might, but instead continued down a long hallway inside the building. The fox was alert, though more relaxed than he'd been in the streets outside; he slid through a brightly-colored curtain, holding it for Geren.

"Why did Zori say my chip was a risk?" Geren asked, in an undertone, once they were out of earshot of the street.

"Nobody has them here." Lysi murmured, stooping to carefully flip a little metal box in the hallway. Finding it empty, he set it against the wall and turned to Geren. "They can be tracked. With the right equipment they answer far off. No one is after you, right?"

"Right," Geren agreed. "But do you know how? Is it like some sort of heterodyne detector?"

"It's . . . not quite like that." The fox turned away and began walking again. "Come."

"So you really do have to barter for showers and food?" Geren asked, trying unsuccessfully to move as quietly as the fox. "You said that, but I didn't really understand. Subsistence is supposed to be a right. A right enforced by the central worlds. Like law and order, and citizen governance, and running water, and datalink access . . . I didn't know it could be this bad."

"Well there are public dispensaries, where bigger ones kill you for food." Lysi's warmth was tantalizing as he slowed his pace to turn back to him, but Geren found his whispered words chilling. "And public showers, where they kill and rape for fun. Usually broken. Rumor has it the plagues come from there."

Geren shook his head, unable to respond. This made him feel mildly disoriented—why would plagues spread from shower facilities?

Why were there plagues at all? Even the term felt archaic, something out of the past, or from colonies with limited medical services during the isolation . . . but certainly nothing that should ever touch a central world during modern times.

What had happened to the society here? How could a central world have reached this level of dysfunction, and why did the rest of the universe not know about it?

Lysi slipped on ahead, oblivious to Geren's internal conflict, and Geren followed apace as they went down a small set of stairs, then made their way through a blackened underground corridor that might once have been a hallway or a tunnel. There was no light, but path the fox followed was well-worn and much traveled, and the synthetic floor was smooth and sandy under Geren's bare paws as the meters passed by in the near-black.

Eventually he realized why some of the designs had seemed vaguely familiar as the hallway opened up into the vestibule of a transit station. Faint light filtered in from street-level gates above a long escalator, and little fires sparkled on the far side of the atrium; the glint of eyes shone from the darkness, silently watching as he and Lysi scurried through a broken door into the offices behind the information counter.

At the factory, they had been completely isolated from the city around them; almost the entire workforce had been brought in from other worlds. The society within had often laughed and joked about the locals, though almost none had ever interacted with them—they were considered an underclass. Uneducated, unintelligent, poor and lazy.

Lesser.

In retrospect, Geren realized he hadn't actually put any thought into those views, accepting without question. And yet the Fonacim were the same genetic stock as any other civilization—but for the fortune of being born on Alaran, he himself could have experienced the same life. Would he have survived? He'd find out, he supposed—though he still felt like a tourist, an observer, the sensation was beginning to erode away, replaced with a burgeoning awareness that he was now as much a part of this underclass as any other citizen.

And that he now had to work and fight to survive, like any other citizen.

He shuddered uncomfortably, licking his lips.

"Maybe Zori and Maven were right," he murmured, then sighed.

Lysi stopped abruptly, turning around and resting a questioning look on Geren.

"Maybe tonight was a good lesson. I will need to find a way to bring something . . . it's only fair."

"You are mine, and I always bring the most," the fox huffed. "I've earned your food for months. More if they knew—"

Geren blinked as the fox cut himself off. He waited a moment for the fox to continue, but nothing was forthcoming. "If they knew what?"

Lysi's eyes shone in the light, and he made a strange, unclassifiable sort of noise. "I can't talk about that."

Geren looked down at the ground; the fox definitely had his secrets.

"But it doesn't matter," Lysi spoke firmly, taking his paw once more, voice earnest. "It's not your fault. Not at all. None of this. You're innocent."

"Since I left the factory, I've survived on the kindness of others . . . I never realized what a gift food could be. One of the door guards at the Niyoz gave me a ration cube, and then . . . Meryka."

"I'm lucky she found you."

"She's Alari, too, you know . . . I know the accent. How did she get here? Was she from the factory, too?"

Lysi hesitated, then shook his head. "Ask any other story," he murmured. "Hers is hers to tell."

Geren nodded again. Lysi tugged him onward, and he stepped around an upturned desk, following the fox's black eartips. Unexpected conversational mines here . . . there was clearly mystery in abundance, but he wasn't sure if he should pry . . . or if he even wanted to know the answers.

"So she asked me a bunch of questions—"

Lysi gave Geren's paw a little warning squeeze, and shook his head.

Geren bit his lip and walked onward.

"This . . . there's this shame," the fox started a few minutes later, then paused again and looked away, slowing his pace and gazing off into space, considering his words. "It—"

A voice rang up from outside a hole in the wall beside them, and Lysi froze, dropping to a silent crouch; Geren, holding his paw, perforce followed.

After a few minutes, the voices faded into the night, never having quite reached intelligibility, and Lysi rose once again, tugging him forward.

"There's a kind of shame that makes us mean," he resumed after a moment, speaking quietly over his shoulder as he crept through the blackness, eyes and teeth glittering in the patches of ambient light from the street outside. "We're weak, afraid. Helpless. So we take it out on each other. Take what we can."

Geren trudged along behind the lithe fox, frowning in the dark. "So, the gun and camo—"

Lysi spun quickly, raising a finger to touch Geren's lips, and he stopped abruptly.

"No. That—please don't talk about that," the fox whispered, ears flicking around. "Not even with me."

Geren bit his lip, rebuked. He drew back, nodding a single nod. "I'm sorry."

"Don't be," Lysi raised his voice to a light, sincere murmur. "It's not your fault. I forgot to say."

A rattle of wind and rain on the soot-caked glass was followed by the subsonic rumble of thunder.

"If it floods again tonight, we'll lose the partrace." Lysi glanced upward as though he could see through the stories above. "The weather gets worse every day."

"Why is that?" Geren stepped carefully, following as the fox turned down another burned-out hallway. Rain misted down through openings in the floors above, coating him with grime and grit.

"I don't know," Lysi murmured. "Not exactly. It's said that the factories do it, that we'll become like Brynton. Through here," he pointed to an exit stair.

As they descended into the very-slightly-lit depths, the signs of environmental encroachment and fire damage grew fewer. While there was little light at first, the door at the bottom had one lonely red lamp shining, which lit the entire hallway behind it.

"The soil is still fertile, they say." Lysi spoke over his shoulder, pushing another curtain out of the way. "Not past no-return yet. We were supposed to all go out of the city tomorrow. To a little garden in the woods."

Geren winced at the sadness in the fox's tone. "Hey . . . I'm sorry about your friends. Will it all be alright?"

"You are not to be sorry." The fox spoke curtly. "I am. I expected better of them."

"But it'll be ok?"

Lysi slowed down, but did not turn or respond.

They came to a black metal door with a small red lamp shining on it. A little sign hung on a nail driven into its center: "Open!"

Lysi rapped four knocks with his knuckle, then waved up at what Geren realized was a video pickup. After a few seconds there was a clunk, and the door was unlocked.

A busty, plump hyena sat on a little stool just inside; Lysi retrieved his token and handed it to her silently. She dropped it into a bucket with a little clink, then grinned, tossing him a clean-looking towel in return.

"Thirty minutes for one, fifteen minutes for two," the guard rasped, voice gravely and rough. She half-closed her eyes and sniffed the air, then cleared her throat and grinned a slow, knowing grin. "But ah . . . if nobody's a-comin', the two of you stay long as you like. Shouldn't be nobody, but I'll knock you up five minutes 'fore, if there is."

Lysi closed his eyes and bowed appreciatively. "Thank you."

"Sure," the guard smiled a snaggletoothed smile.

Lysi ushered Geren past her and through another door; he found himself in a blue-lit room with a tiled floor. The fox's firm paw on his rump kept him moving forward, even as the other paw began peeling off his filthy cloak and underwear. By the time they neared the end of the little hallway, Geren was nude, and the explorations of Lysi's paws were making it difficult for him to walk. Another paw against his upper back pressed him against the cool wall, and his hunger was momentarily forgotten as a soft, warm pawpad stroked firmly against his rump and hot breath stirred the fur on the back of his neck.

A small control panel sat beside a blue steel door in the same wall, and Lysi reluctantly lifted his paw from Geren's back to tap on it. Soft hissing began to emanate from behind the door, and the fox returned to Geren, sliding black-furred paws down to his hips and latching on.

Geren closed his eyes and tilted his head back with an appreciative murmur; teeth closed gently on the joint of his neck and shoulder in a possessive bite, and the fox ground firmly against his rump, hot breath wafting through his neckfur.

He had never felt remotely as desired in all his years with Alain. His heart beat quickly, and he pressed himself against the wall, closing his eyes and groaning softly at the warmth of the fox plastered against him.

"In," Lysi whispered, drawing back and turning Geren's hips towards the door. Geren fumbled with the handle for a moment, then found the release and swung it inward. A blast of steam and hot, wet air rushed past him, but the fox urged him forward.

Inside, multiple jets of water sprayed, steamed and misted into a dimly lit but surprisingly clean and well-maintained little chamber; Lysi pushed him in eagerly, closing the door behind them. The delightful sensation of hot water coursing through his fur sucked away Geren's attention momentarily; in the next moment, Lysi had pulled a brush and some soap from a rack on the wall and was brushing lather firmly through his chestfur.

He sighed softly and raised his arms, muzzle falling open in sensual pleasure as Lysi explored his form with the brush. When he was fully soaped up at last, the fox stood back up and touched noses with him briefly, then stole a little kiss of his lips, placing the brush into Geren's paw.

Needing no further direction, Geren began to thoroughly clean his foxy lover, paws tracing along behind the brush, surprised at the many ridges of scars beneath his fur on his back and hips; after Lysi's first few little twitches, he softened his strokes.

As he made his way down to the fox's thighs, trying for the moment to ignore his more lascivious impulses, a black-furred paw settled to his head, stroking clawtips through his hair. After a moment, the fox sank before him, kneeling to warmly lap his muzzle as the water streamed down on them, rinsing their fur and hair.

"My yotie," the fox whispered, then kissed him. Geren melted into the moment, and pressed back, tongue lapping and exploring the fox's muzzle. For time interminable they made out under the hot water, at once rinsing their fur and soaking up heat from the water—and each other—neither seeming to want more than the other's loving attentions.

The moment was finally broken by a sharp rap on the outer door.

Lysi rose to his feet, surprisingly lithe. He smiled coyly, tugging Geren up with him; after returning the brushes and soap to the rack, he gathered him up in a tight embrace, slowly turning with him under the spray, nose to nose.

"I love you, Lysi," Geren whispered, then winced self-consciously, looking away with a little shake of his head. "Wait . . . what I mean . . . I mean—"

"Ssh," Lysi whispered. The clawtips of one of his paws dug gently into Geren's hips, and he raised the other paw to his chin, lifting it to gaze into his eyes once more. They turned for a while longer in silence before the fox finally spoke.

"You talk too much," the fox spoke. "I hope what you mean is what you said, because I love you, too, yotie."

Geren twisted his muzzle away and trembled softly, paws clutching at Lysi's hips.

"I've claimed you as mine," Lysi murmured huskily. "My property. And I won't ever let go. I didn't know, when I saw you . . ." He paused for a moment, looking away thoughtfully, then turned back, somber. "Geren, it's dangerous here. It's all . . . going downhill. I don't know how I've survived this far. I—I'm a . . . I . . ."

"Yes?" Geren prodded.

"I . . ." Lysi looked torn. After a breath, he sighed and shook his head. "I can't promise you a long, happy life. I can't promise to protect you. Or me."

In that moment, for the first time, Geren realized that Lysi saw in him the same lifeline he saw in the fox.

"But I was the one sinking," he whispered, slightly stunned by the realization. He shook himself, then drew in a breath to explain his odd statement, but the fox interrupted him again by caressing his whiskers.

"Ssh. You were trying to stay afloat." Lysi's whiskers twitched, and he leaned back to push open the door of the shower room. "I was . . . in a way, I was trying to stay under. I've lost some good . . . friends, this year. Too many.

I've had to do terrible things. When I found that little hole, the one in the wall? I wasn't up there looking for beauty."

Geren's breath caught.

"I'd seen so much death, so much helplessness, you know?"

"Will you hope, fox? For me?"

"You came back. You came to sink below the surface with me." Lysi's wide-eyes blinked again, and a little smile touched his lips. "A little hope, I can do."

"'Sometimes,'" Geren murmured, touching noses with the fox, "as someone wise once told me, 'the cost of freedom must be stolen from your pocket.'"

Outside, Lysi dried him first, then himself, then threw the clothes and towel into a chute in the wall and closed the door.

Another rap sounded on the panel, a bit more urgent.

Geren tilted his head, glancing worriedly towards the door, but Lysi merely smiled a reassuring smile.

With a little chime, a bin opened beside the chute. Lysi reached in and emerged with their clothes; they appeared clean and smelled sanitized. Geren reached for the cloak, but Lysi shook his head, stealing it playfully from his grasp.

"Let me," the fox murmured, and began to dress Geren himself. Slowly, lovingly the fox slid his own underwear up Geren's tawny-furred thighs, then wrapped the now-softened cloak about his shoulders, finishing with a soft kiss atop his muzzle.

"Now me," the fox whispered, lifting a hindpaw; Geren knelt, sliding the leg loop around Lysi's black-furred footpaw; the fox stepped in, then lifted his other leg, allowing Geren to pull them all the way up and snap the waistband around his tailbase.

Geren sighed and stood, watching raptly as Lysi pulled the coveralls on, concealing a body he very much wanted uncovered. As he turned for the door, he was surprised to feel the fox's paws slide around his chest and hold him in place.

"When we get home," Lysi's breathy whisper was right in Geren's ear, "I'm going to show you're mine. I'm going to teach you some of the things only foxes know."

Geren's knees nearly buckled, and he whined softly in response.

As they left the shower room, Geren could swear that the guard and the lanky panther waiting to enter were both smirking at them. In reply, Lysi tugged him back again for a possessive little earkiss. He felt a strange sensation course through him, and it made him feel very small and very possessed.

It was wonderful.

They walked underground for a long time, finally exiting in a completely different area than the one they'd entered. The little storm door opened outward from a concrete slab, and they both paused under the overhang as they discovered that the storm had truly turned forth its fury upon the city.

It took a few moments of building up confidence before they set out into its driving rain, immediately paw-deep in reeking, silty mud. They worked their way back to the same route as before, but Geren barely recognized it, transformed by runnels of water in the street and frequent lightning.

They had only made it about halfway when the power went out completely, and the sparse street lighting snapped off, leaving them stumbling forward for a few minutes before their eyes adjusted.

Flickers and flashes of lightning were blinding, and the wind roared through the streets, carrying with it debris and rain. The weir they had crossed before was now an ominous, roaring flood, and they were forced to detour several kilometers out of the way to cross an equipment bridge upstream; even then, water lapped only meters below the narrow span.

Geren wrapped Lysi's waterlogged cloak tightly around him, shivering softly as he followed the fox across. Only the promise of foxy warmth kept him from diving into an alcove on the other side to avoid the pounding rain.

When at last they reentered Lysi's tenement building, they stood shivering in the atrium for some time, silent and dripping, as if shocked by the ferocity of the weather.

"We're going to lose the partrace," Lysi sighed, breaking the silence at last.

"What is the partrace?"

"The lower fifth of the city. It's along the river, where the poor live."

Geren had already nodded half a nod before Lysi's words sank in.

Where the poor live.

"Well, nevermind," Lysi shook his head, with a tiny flash of what Geren almost thought was a predatory grin. "Nothing we can do. Come."

Geren obediently followed the fox back to his room, shaking softly.

The door wasn't even shut before the fox urged him forward with a warm paw on his rump; he could hear Lysi's excited, aroused breathing behind him as he was guided to the support column in the middle of the room, and stripped down.

Despite his dizzying hunger, Geren's body responded immediately to the fox's touch. He found himself arching, breathing stilled, ears flat against his head as the fox began to explore him with his muzzle, nuzzling and lapping hotly through his soaked fur.

Trembling with urgency, Lysi's paws found Geren's hips and turned him around, then pushed him down until his back was pressed against the gritty floor.

The fox was much stronger than he looked; his black paws found and held Geren's wrists, pressing them down behind his head with a warm, lusty growl.

Geren offered no resistance as the fox lapped along his throat, nibbling and nuzzling, his own breathing quick with need. He watched through half-closed eyes as Lysi kicked off his coveralls, then laid his head back in happy surrender.

A little smile of pure happiness touched his lips.

A loud bang and a flurry of motion startled him up; Lysi's knee dragged across his face as the fox rose even faster.

"What—" Geren blinked blurry eyes up at the sound of a soft thud, watching in shock as the fox was flung back into his kitchen table by a looming form silhouetted in the doorway.

Lysi lay still in the wreckage and did not move.

"Ugh." A gruff, angry, familiar voice caused Geren's stomach to knot. "This is exactly what I meant by before you get in trouble."

"No!" Geren cried out, struggling to his feet. "Stop! D-don't hurt him."

"Looks like I already did," Lapis' voice was scornful as he regarded the crumpled form, then fractionally more solicitous as he turned to Geren. "Are you hurt?"

"No! No, he—"

"Good. I'm gonna take you home."

"No!" Geren screamed, stumbling to check on the fox, breathless and terrified.

A disgusted sigh from the geared-up wolf was followed by a firm grip on the scruff of his neck, and he was dragged back toward the door. Geren twisted around and struck out, trying to escape or inflict damage, unsure of which drive was stronger; all his thoughts were on the silent, folded body just meters away.

His blows were ineffectual, and one firm backhand across his jaw from the wolf spun him around, leaving him stunned and weak.

"Fucking idiot," Lapis growled. "I'm trying to save you, and this is what I get? You're just gonna cause me trouble, aren't you?"

Nearly a hundred and thirty kilograms of wolf twisted him over and wrenched his arms up behind him; something hard and tight encircled his legs and wrists, then they were drawn painfully together. Geren's heartsick scream was cut off as a strap was wrapped around his muzzle, and then Lapis tossed him over his shoulder like he might a duffel.

As he was hauled out of the door, the last thing he saw through tear-blurred eyes was Lysi's inert form, blood highlighting the white fur beneath his lovely jawline.

Sixth

OUTSIDE OF THE BUILDING, THE RAIN FELL in a nearly solid wall, washing Geren's tears into the broken concrete and dirt. Around the corner of the building was a little security runabout; as they approached, its rear hatch swung open, and the wolf tossed Geren through, closing it firmly behind him.

Geren stared out helplessly through the side window as the wolf picked his way through flooded streets before coming to a guarded stile across a wall of sandbags; once cleared through the checkpoint and across the stile, the roads were suddenly far cleaner and there was less destruction and disorder; Geren recognized it as the same area Meryka had taken him through.

Lapis drove on. The many rings of lights spanning the immense factory cast an ominous glow over the streets, creating a sickly orange dusk from night, growing brighter the closer they came to its monstrous walls. The bustle of the outer village eventually died down and gave way to increasingly quiet suburbs.

A column of bright white floods on the road proved to be yet another gated checkpoint, and Lapis dutifully slowed to a stop as the guard approached, cloak drawn up tight against the heavy rain.

A wild hope sprung up within Geren, and he writhed himself into a sitting position, then began banging himself against the back hatch, mmphing for all he was worth.

In response, a hand-light was abruptly directed through Lapis' back window.

Geren squinting into the harsh light, eyes wide, ears flat, trying to look as distressed as he felt.

"You got yourself a cute one, sir," the male voice behind the light sounded distinctly like a young canid. "Good coat on him, too . . . looks healthy and well-fed. High-class local?"

Geren sank back into the seat and closed his eyes.

"Naw," Lapis growled back, amused. "Well, sort-of. Terminated factory worker. Tried going local, looks like, but I promised to look out for him, so I'm bringing him back."

The hand-light flicked off, and Geren closed his eyes against the afterimage.

"Nice. That's a real nice deal. Was there currency involved?"

There was a momentary pause, then a nasty chuckle, but Geren was still blinded from the light and couldn't see the exchange.

"Right. Well, welcome home. Enjoy."

"Oh you know I will," Lapis rumbled darkly. "Don't be too jealous. Don't know if he's picked up any of the local . . . ah . . . culture."

"Ah." The guard's voice sounded disappointed, then tilted mischievously upwards. "Well, here's hoping not. And, ah . . . sir . . ."

"Find your own!" Lapis laughed. "Good night."

"Night, sir!"

Lapis pulled away and they were off once more, bouncing over the road until they came to a set of walled-off cottages.

Once the wolf unloaded him and untied his legs and muzzle, Geren let his weight settle limply to the ground.

When commanded to walk, he sat on the half-flooded sidewalk in the driving rain and would not move. When dragged by his hair, he twisted and whimpered in pain, but did not relent.

When at last, cursing and soaked, Lapis undid his broad belt and threatened him with it as he lay on the ground, Geren spat at his feet.

It didn't have the effect he'd anticipated.

Rather than beating him, the wolf merely sighed and stuffed the belt into his pocket.

Grasping him by the scruff of the neck, Lapis lifted his feet with his other paw and carried him through the gate, which shut behind him with an authoritative 'thunk'.

"C'mon, boy," the wolf rumbled. "You're not a local. You're civilized. Educated. This isn't who you are. You don't belong with that rabble, and they won't accept you. That little worm just wanted degrade you. Happens all the time here to your type, believe me. I've seen it. He would have taken everything you had and left you in the street with a slit throat."

"No!" Geren yelled, so firm that Lapis jumped and stopped under the eaves of the little cottage, frowning down at him. "Not Lysi. Not ever." He swallowed a sob that threatened to consume him. "Please. You do what you want to me, but at least go check on him. Please . . . he could be hurt."

"Don't be so stupid, boy. You weren't out there more than a week—you don't know how it works. Locals here, they aren't the same as people, you gotta understand. They're parasites—bottom-feeders. No morals, no nothin'. I've been here ten years, I've seen it all. And anyway, look, I hit that fox real hard when he came at me—folded him right up and he went down head-first. Wasn't breathing when we left, probably broke his skull."

Geren jammed his eyes shut and shook his head; more sobs rose from his belly, and what little fight remained in him trickled away into a nauseated whimper.

Lapis snorted, then tapped his paw against the door-plate. The door swung open on a darkened little cottage with barred, shuttered windows; with another sigh, he hauled Geren through the doorframe and dropped him onto the floor of the main room, paw still tight around his scruff, then kicked the door shut behind him.

"Listen here, you're safe from all that, now—your ex thought we'd do well together."

"Alain?" Geren felt only slightly more ill. "This was his idea?"

The wolf folded his arms across his chest, frowning down at him. "Mm. Now, listen . . . I promised I would take care of you, but you've been a damn handful already. I called up Paulie, from the plant—you might remember her? I didn't know what state I'd find you in . . . but I can smell. Now I've gotta get you tested for all the category C's—if you're not clean, well . . . there'll be hell to pay."

Geren lifted his head, baring his teeth in canine defiance. "Well sorry to disappoint you, but I don't think I am, because I don't think he was, and we made love."

"Feh." Lapis released him, shoving him away with his hindpaw. His nose was wrinkled in revulsion. "By the gods."

Geren rolled onto his face, wet eyes pressed against the floor.

"Well, you'll regret that. Thought you'd be smarter." Lapis' voice was solemn. He drew a flask from his hip and took a swig, then wiped his lips with the back of a paw. "Thought you'd be a cute partner, too. Hell, I still do . . . but I grew up on a world with slaves, and so I know how to keep one, one way or another."

Geren cracked an eyelid, staring back up at him. "Slaves? That's . . . that's—"

"Now me," The wolf interrupted, then snorted. "I have ways to get my fun no matter what you got. So if you refuse me, we'll just go a different way."

"I do not consent to this," Geren spoke, voice almost a whisper. "I am not property."

"Yeah, you are. Mine. And there's nobody stronger than me to take you away."

"How can you be so evil?"

"Evil?" Lapis paused, staring down at him with a baffled expression. "You think I'm evil? I'm one of the good guys. I'm not evil, I'm just trying to protect your stupid ass."

Geren was speechless.

Lapis turned to a wall fixture and began rummaging through it, emerging with a bulky, wide collar. "A little present for you. Whatever you do, oh please don't fight."

Geren shrank away from the approaching wolf.

His weak show of resistance was just that, and a few seconds of squirming and growling later he heard the collar's lock snick shut behind his head.

Closing his eyes, Geren slumped in atavistic resignation, passively allowing his weight to settle against the floor as the wolf pushed him onto his back.

"Don't do what I say, and I'll give you a shock until you behave. You're good? I feed you, and maybe I'm nicer. You're bad? This is the least of what I've got to hurt you with. You're here now, so you better get used to it—I don't want to hear complaining, got it? We keep it simple. Bathroom's behind you—you have it completely clean before Paulie shows up or you get worse."

Geren had barely finished by the time the doorchime sounded; wordlessly, Lapis clipped a leash onto his collar and led him to his guest as she unpacked a medical kit.

Looking up through crusty eyelashes, Geren recognized the broad-shouldered grey wolf as one of the Cerion staff physicians from his wing.

She looked him over dispassionately, then pulled a set of black gloves up over her elbows.

"Yeah, I've seen this one before." Paulie's voice was a bit gruff, and she cleared her throat. "Hope he doesn't have the local lordalychidae, or we'll each have to do a turn in the scrubber. Stuff's nasty . . . has some sort of toxin that causes dissolution of the neural sheathing. That one wasn't one of ours, so we're not immunized against it. Hold him down."

Geren's protests were ignored; with unnecessary strength, Lapis forced him against the floor.

Despite his pain, something stuck in his head.

One of ours?

Treating him like a piece of meat, Pauli methodically extracted samples from all over him, then carefully began scanning his whole body with a small device until it cheeped.

For a few minutes, she manipulated his data on her pad, then frowned at the results, eyes widening.

"That little bastard survived the Denian plague."

"Yeah?" Lapis scowled. "All the factory workers were immunized."

"No, you idiot," The other wolf snorted, eyes flicking back and forth as she swiped through results. "Not this one. The local. The fox. I analyzed his traces, and they show signs of conditioned immunity. Distinct positive response from Denian IV antigens. Intelligence will want to collect his body for analysis."

"Intelligence?" Lapis' hackles, which had risen at her initial words, settled quickly back down, and his eyebrows drew down in concern. "Why? It wasn't supposed to kill them all . . ."

"It was made to be selective, not survivable. If he was infected, he should have died."

"So?"

"So," Pauli straightened, sounding irritated by Lapis' failure to follow, "that fox wasn't immunized—he was cured of a disease made to be incurable without our stuff. Our stuff is carefully controlled. Ergo hey, either he's one of ours or there are people out there with stuff way beyond the level of medical science that's supposed to be left here."

"Lady, I really don't care about all that."

"Well," Pauli said, drawing the sound out as if summoning patience, "just give me the fox's flat later so I can collect him, ok? If he's one of ours, he's obviously deep cover, so no foul."

"Fine. So what about this one?"

"He's clean. Completely. A few social viruses ... the residual complement from his home planet, and a few harmless locals we've all got. From his catabolic state, I'd say he's hungry. Other than that, and a slight propensity for arthritis in old age if left unaddressed, he's good to go. I'll let our friend know, if you want."

Geren glanced up at Lapis, who seemed instantly more smug, devouring him with his eyes.

"Yeah. Yeah, do let him know. Tell him, ah ... something came up, and he wants to stay. Completely clean, huh? Guess I won't be needing you, after all."

"Sure, sure." Pauli's teeth showed in a lupine grin. Her nose wrinkled a bit, though Geren couldn't tell whether her expression was disgust or pity. "Try not to break him too bad, ok?"

"I hear coyotes are tough. We'll see." The wolf gazed appraisingly down at Geren. "I bet I get him broken in pretty quick."

"You're incorrigible. I always took you for a secret romantic. No?"

Lapis snorted, eyes glinting as he regarded her. "Since you mention it ..."

"Well," warmth washed into her voice, "if you ever want more of a social call ..."

Geren averted his eyes in disgust at their coy interplay; somewhere in the hellscape that was the city, Lysi's orange fur lay stretched out in the rubble of his ruined but loving little life, barely cool. The thought of those beautiful, honey-colored eyes open, unseeing, drained of their quiet intelligence made him nauseous.

"Yeah, I miss those." Lapis was saying. "You around for a while, then?"

"I don't know," the female wolf rumbled, shifting to an uncertain murmur. There was a rustle, and she moved away, packing away her kit. "I figure if we go back to Brynton, we'll probably go together . . . right?"

"Brynton?" Lapis' voice lifted slightly in surprise. "You don't think the rumors are true, do you? You think we're pulling out?"

"Bluntly, yes. I'm guessing, but you know how my guesses are. Possibly even by the end of the year. So like I said, if we all end up on the same ship back home, you won't want anything too visible . . ."

"Oh . . . and so you think they might go there, too. I got it now," Lapis growled, apparently enlightened. Geren jumped in surprise as the wolf patted his rear, then ruffled his hair. "It's alright. He gave him to me, and you know I take care of my things. Especially gifts."

"Gifts . . . ha. That's not . . . exactly . . . legal here, you know." Pauli rose.

"Yeah but possession and all. And I'm the law, so . . ."

The two wolves shared a conspiratorial smirk.

As the they walked to the doorway making their farewells, Geren curled up around his paws. Another round of sobs started as convulsive clenching in his gut before rising to take over; tears soaked the fur beneath his eyes and dampened his cheeks.

A devastating sense of loss hung over him and nothing else could get through. The sneaking suspicion Alain had sold him out, the shockingly casual mention of what sounded like biological warfare against the Fonaci citizenry . . . but mostly the shock of losing the fox. A morass of sick sorrow rendered him completely dead inside, worse than he'd ever felt.

Despite their incredibly brief association, Lysi had made him feel special in a way he'd never felt capable of before, and had buffered him from the collapse of his existence and given him something to live for.

Now there was only emptiness, infinitely worse than it had been.

Watching Lapis close the door and set its locks, Geren was unable to even summon the hatred and anger he knew he should feel when looking at his abductor and captor . . . who had killed the fox he loved.

He just felt numb and empty, as though more of his spirit drained from him with each exhalation.

"I'm sorry, Lyss," Geren sighed, nearly silent. He hung his head as the wolf paced slowly towards him.

"Up." The wolf snapped. Geren stood—there was little else to do.

"Good boy. I want you in my bed tonight," Lapis growled. "Are you coming as my good boy, or as my slave?"

Geren turned hollow eyes to Lapis, thoughts oozing like cold grease.

"Boy," Lapis held out his right paw, "Or slave?" He lifted the leash in his left.

"I don't care," Geren said at last, feeling fatigued beyond measure.

"Let's start nice, then," Lapis said, then leaned forward and kissed him roughly. It wasn't pleasant, and Geren didn't return it; he simply opened his muzzle and let the wolf take what he wanted. Moments later, Lapis broke free and turned him towards the single bedroom in the low cottage.

Unlike Lysi, there was nothing subtle or passionate about Lapis' interests; strange gear hung from the walls, strange looking furniture was scattered around the room, and there was a cage at the side of the bed that was adorned with a comically thick locking device.

Noticing his glance, the wolf smirked and smacked his rump. "That's your bed. Now, shall we start with where that fox left off?"

Geren couldn't summon the will to resist as the wolf latched his paws to solid cuffs attached to the bed. Lapis wrapped a strap around his muzzle, then pressed a set of synthetic caps onto his sharper teeth, rendering them blunt.

"Good boy." Lapis smirked, inspecting his handiwork. Apparently satisfied, he began to undress himself, then swung back onto the bed and rose to his knees, devouring Geren with his eyes.

"I know this is all sudden, but you'll learn to like it," the wolf said with a lick of his lips and a smile that didn't fit his face. He reached out a paw to squeeze Geren's muzzle, then slapped his cheek softly. "You're mine now, and I'll treat you good as long as you act good."

For hours, Geren wordlessly endured the wolf's rough affections, just waiting for the wolf to be done with him. For hours after Lapis had finished and fallen to sleep on top of him, he lay beneath the wolf's heavy form, wheezing for breath.

Everything Lapis knew about sex was cliché, Geren reflected; the bondage, the dirty talk, the play. There was no passion, no ingenuity, no desire. It all felt so predictable that he figured Lapis had been watching much of the same type of material that he had.

Years ago, even weeks ago, the thought of being the bottom for someone like Lapis had been a darkest, deepest fantasy.

Now, the reality brought not the slightest hint of arousal—all he could think of was Lysi.

Eventually, despite hunger, anguish and pain, a restless, uncomfortable sleep claimed him.

The next morning, Lapis woke him with a soft nudge and dragged him into the shower. An hour later, as the wolf prepared to leave, he gave Geren an extensive list of house-work and told him the locations of the cleaning supplies.

"So this place will sparkle when I return, right?"

"Yeah," Geren muttered, hanging his head.

"'Yes sir,'" Lapis snapped.

"Yes sir," Geren whispered, though it made him feel nau-seous to obey.

"Much better. I better be blown away by how nice this place looks, with all day to work on it. Do you cook?"

"No. I am . . . I was . . . an engineer," Geren said softly.

"Well . . . tomorrow I'll find some education programs on it. I'll need you to have dinner ready for me when I get home from work."

"Yes sir," Geren whispered meekly.

Lapis eyed him for a moment, then nodded and left with a bounce in his step.

When the wolf came home ten hours later, he reeked of sweat, and there were spatters of dried blood in his fur and on his armor. He blew in like a storm, but paused just inside the door, eyes narrowing.

Geren cowered in the doorway to the kitchen, watching. His paws hurt from cleaning, and he was wheezing from the dust that he'd kicked up.

"Boy! Come here," the wolf growled, pushing the door gently shut behind him and leaning against the wall.

Overriding his instincts to hide, Geren forced his legs to carry him into the room, tail tucked, eyes down.

"Sir?"

"Had a rough day. Help me get my boots off."

The wolf raised his hindpaws one at a time, and Geren gingerly unbuckled his big, armored boots, sliding them off and setting them beside the door with trembling paws.

"This looks good," Lapis rumbled, squinting a bit as he looked around. "Better than I expected. Nice to come home to a clean house."

He sounded tired.

Geren lowered his head, uncertain of what sort of response to make.

"Look . . . we've got off to a bad start, me and you," the wolf sighed, flopping into his chair and leaning back. "I was just thinking today . . . me, I grew up on a slave planet. Was a drover for a while. It just . . . it all comes natural, I guess. And all this, I thought it'd be fun, you know? Alain said you'd like it like this."

"Alain never understood me," Geren said, voice hoarse. "It's different when it's real. It's different after Lysi."

The wolf winced, absently plucking at his work gloves, worrying them off.

"I get it," Lapis started, before the silence could become awkward. "I get it. You liked that fox. Maybe I was wrong about him, but he's dead. This is your home now."

"I don't . . ." Geren started, then bit his lip. He didn't want to strain the wolf's sudden magnanimity.

Lapis tossed his gloves to the floor, then pulled his flask free from his jacket pocket, unscrewing the top and taking an extended swig. After wiping his lips, he took Geren's chin softly in his paw, lifting it up and gazing into his eyes.

"Look, maybe it's not what you want, but . . . let's make the best of it. Be my partner. You keep the house going . . . cook, clean, that sort of thing. I keep you safe. Don't even have to play rough like last night if you don't want."

Geren looked away and closed his eyes; the thought of Lysi's face chilled what little warmth rose within him. He pressed his lips together and said nothing, sickened by the reality of sliding inexorably into this poor excuse for a life.

Just weeks ago, he had thought himself ordinarily happy, with a good job, a boyfriend, what he thought to be a reasonable amount tucked away in savings, and a clear path forward.

It seemed a lifetime in the past—a dream misremembered, from which he had fallen upon waking, tumbling haplessly through nearly his full gamut of emotions to arrive here—here, where his sole remaining chance at contentment was constrained to morsels of praise and goodwill from one who regarded him as nothing more than an object.

All he could think of was Lysi's restrained warmth, his nimble grace.

He raised his head and looked up at the exhausted Lapis, finally recognizing the tiny, confused emotion that tweaked his heavy brow.

For all his bulk and brawn, for all his strength and bluster...the wolf was just as afraid of rejection as Geren had been.

"I want you to let me go," he stated, locking eyes with his captor. "I can't ever live like this. We'll call it good, and I'll walk way. That's all."

"Eh?" Lapis flinched back, teeth pressed together.

"Please, just let me go. You can't keep me here—it's not fair. It's not right. I don't want to be your partner, mate, or slave. You can do what you like to me tonight, tomorrow...but please...promise you'll let me go...soon?" Geren's voice trembled with fear.

The wolf gazed down at him for a while, expression slowly cooling from hurt to a mask of bone-chilling indifference. Geren grew weaker with each passing moment, wanting to fall at the wolf's feet and beg forgiveness; the only thing that kept him standing was his memory of Lysi, and the knowledge that he was facing his killer.

Lapis rocked to his feet, reaching forward to clutch his collar. He slowly lifted him upward, then leaned in until they were nose to nose, his eyes fixed on Geren's.

"No."

"Please," Geren wrapped thin paws around wide lupine wrists, his voice strained. "Why not?"

The wolf tightened his grip.

"Promised your ex."

"He couldn't want . . . this," Geren's voice was thin from the pressure on his larynx.

Lapis flinched again. "This is for your own good!"

"It's killing me inside."

"Just for now!" Lapis protested, then dropped him, shoving him backwards onto the floor and raising his paws in exasperation, sounding aggrieved. "Food and medical care. Safety. Warm, clean place to sleep, just like the factory—a good home. On this planet, that's luxury! You'll grow to appreciate it, mark my words."

"I won't," Geren said, then shook his head. "I need to be free."

"Agh," Lapis growled, then reached down to grab him by the scruff once more, the last of his nascent benevolence evaporating as he lifted him roughly to his feet.

"I didn't mean to hurt you," Geren felt his voice rise in fear.

Lapis' grip tightened, and his eyes widened. "Hurt? Me? Don't be stupid. You can't hurt me—I do the hurting here."

Geren dug his feet in as the wolf began to drag him towards his bedroom, but he was by far the weaker of the two, and soon he found himself face down on the bed once more.

He didn't even bother resisting as he was locked in place.

"Hungry?" Lapis' voice was close, fetid breath wafting across his muzzle. "Too bad. You get nothing until you apologize and beg to stay. You were so good earlier, cleaning up like that. Shame you ruined it all. Now I've gotta punish you."

Geren felt his tail roughly lifted out of the way. He knew what was coming, but he had no intention of giving

Lapis the satisfaction of reacting; he took a big mouthful of pillow and bit down hard, squeezing his eyes shut and bracing himself.

The first blow of the belt was far more painful than he'd expected, and he twitched in anticipation of the second, ears back to listen to his tormentor. The second blow fell across his rump in the same spot as the first, and pain coruscated through him. The third brought his eyes open once more, and the fourth had him straining against this metal bonds, teeth poking holes in the stiff pillowcase.

The fifth and sixth had his heart pounding in his throat, and on the seventh he yelped, trying to writhe away but unable to gain purchase. The eighth, ninth and tenth brought more yelps and barks of pain and fear; by the fifteenth he was whimpering and spluttering constantly.

On the eighteenth, he let go of his bitehold and screamed out, his light muscles straining against his restraints. Lapis laughed a nasty little laugh, as if excited by his breaking.

The walls rang as the wolf began to whip him faster, each hard blow following quickly upon the last. When at last Geren broke down, sobbing and crying and begging incoherently for him to stop, his reprieve was only momentary.

Mercilessly, relentlessly, Lapis beat him, as if working out his own pain and hurt with each stroke. By the time the wolf subsided and tossed his belt to the side, Geren was hoarse and nauseous, warm and blurry with endorphins, voice reduced to a little ragged mewl.

"Lots to say. Didn't get most of it—You were trying to say you were sorry, right?" Lapis rubbed his rump roughly.

"Yes! Yes," Geren blathered, ears flat.

Another crushing blow between his legs nearly made him vomit.

"Sir."

"Yessir, yessir," Geren gurgled.

"Making progress," Lapis tried to sound smug, but missed it by a shade. "Now it's time to fuck."

The nights grew longer as winter set in with a vengeance over the next few months, bringing with it, Lapis told him, record cold temperatures that he should be thankful to not have to be out in.

The wolf's treatment gradually softened again as time went on, and Geren found himself falling into a daily routine of cleaning, cooking, and enduring.

Cooking, of all things, had proven the best distraction; despite his initial misgivings—and his father's line about engineers and cooking being like acid and alkali—he'd discovered in himself a knack for it. It kept his mind busy, and his paws occupied . . . and Lapis certainly seemed increasingly pleased by his progress.

Now and again, Lapis would return injured or filthy from some action gone wrong, and Geren would have to tend to his wounds and repair his gear. One day he came in reeking of a familiar, awful smell, and Geren sucked in his breath, instantly recalling his conversation with Meryka.

"That smells like effluent," he noted cautiously. "Was there a leak?"

"Goddamn terrorists," Lapis growled, slamming his gauntlet gloves down on the table and ripping off his armor. "The whole damn factory is down for who-knows-how-long. They even bombed the goddamn shuttle, right on the launch. Destroyed the pad, killed a bunch of execs. Can't get parts or people in, and they got every damn able body wading around in that crap. Say it ain't toxic, but . . ."

"Oh it's toxic," Geren tried to keep the interest out of his tone. "You're gonna look like you have mange if you don't wash it off."

"We took showers afterwards."

"Won't help. You need a mild acid bath. I can probably make one."

Lapis eyed him suspiciously for a moment, then nodded. "I guess you'd know. Fine. Get to work."

Geren almost enjoyed the opportunity to use his chemistry knowledge once again. After reassuring Lapis that there was plenty of time, he began to inventory all the various cleaners, solvents. It took about an hour of checking and cross-checking for adverse reactions from secondary ingredients, but eventually he arrived at a set of combinants that he decided should achieve his purpose, with a little work.

As he was measuring out two of the cleaners he planned to catalyze with a piece of chain, it suddenly occurred to him that he might be able to make something quite a lot stronger. He pondered for a moment, looking over his list. It was there—he had enough on-hand to cook up an extremely caustic mixture. It would at least cause Lapis severe burns, and probably enable him to escape.

He could easily blind the wolf, at the very least, and from there . . .

After reflecting on it for a moment, he sighed, staring sadly down at his paws.

He could never do it.

No matter how much he hated the wolf, that sort of cruelty was on a different level entirely; with another sigh, he finished his bath and diluted it down to a safe strength.

As if he could read his thoughts, Lapis first made him test the solution on himself.

When Geren showed no symptoms after a little while, he reluctantly settled into the big tub.

Geren settled in with a brush, bucket, and goggles, and began cleaning. After a few minutes, his captor began to settle down, and started telling him about all the little attacks and probes his security teams had dealing with over the past few weeks.

"It seems random, but it's hard to tell. Can't find a pattern, and they're not going after the big stuff ... not until this today. Don't even know how they got in, but they turned the pipes back in on the subfloor, which was supposed to be hermetic. All hell's broke loose down there now."

"That's creative," Geren murmured appreciatively, working through Lapis' thighfur. "Who do you think was behind it?"

"It's gotta be the competition. Locals ain't up to that, and there's all kinds of unrest down south, too. They're hitting our profits."

Ah, the competition.

They always heard about 'the competition', and how they needed to remain cost-competitive. The invisible bogey-man, hiding behind every deal, listening on every unsecured channel ... but now, more than ever, Geren was sure they didn't actually exist. Something was very rotten about every single piece of the operation, and he felt stupid for how long he'd believed.

Right up until the end.

Still, Lapis' comment about the locals stuck in his head.

Lysi, he reflected, had seemed both organized and intelligent; as a window into his culture, he showed a view of his people that belied Lapis' assertion. And ... he tensed, struck by a realization—Lysi knew Meryka well, and Meryka ...

Had the foxes been working together?

"Why don't you think it's the locals?" he probed.

"Eh? Feck. Locals are too busy trying to survive."

"Oh," Geren said, then dared, "Is that because our plagues and stuff keep them like that?"

"Yeah," Lapis scratched his neck boredly, and Geren worked his way up to the wolf's hips, careful to avoid his genitalia. "The last one worked well ... real effective. Anyway, this attack, whoever did that, it took coordination, and locals ain't got that anymore."

Geren bit his lip, staring at the back of Lapis' head, but kept his paws moving.

Such a casual confession to such a horrible crime. His stomach roiled, and suddenly he felt a strong urge to dissolve the lot of them for what they'd done. From the sounds of it, Lysi had improbably survived one of their worst plagues, only to die at the hand of Lapis . . . who didn't even know—or care—who he'd killed.

"What's up?" Lapis turned to look back at him, and he realized that he'd stopped cleaning.

"Sorry . . . just thinking of the last time I had to do an effluent purge. It's nasty stuff."

Hastily, he resumed, mind churning on.

Perhaps it was time to purge a different sort of effluent.

He stared at the back of Lapis' head.

He'd been too close to see it, too blinded by overwhelming emotions, but now, examined clearly, it seemed obvious that there had been much more to the fox than he'd known to look for. And he'd betrayed him by attracting Lapis; his mere presence had destroyed what plagues, famine, flood and fire had not.

Tears began soaking the fur around his eyes, eventually running down his muzzle to fall into the alkaline rinse bucket below.

Perhaps, he reflected, he should just dissolve himself; he was cursed, and the world felt impossibly cruel.

The crushing depression Geren struggled with left him almost relieved of thought, like some safety valve that had opened under pressure.

Conversation between him and Lapis eventually became simple, and, oddly, almost convivial; the primitive side of him was warmed by the wolf's increasing kindness and praise. Somehow, he found a twisted sort of happy place in the midst of hell, and buried away the parts of him that were screaming.

Routine, routine, routine.

Routine distracted him from high-order thoughts. Routine gave him something to be at any given moment, led him from one path to the next, and routine brought him surcease from the pain. Routine was the perfect diversion from thoughts of what might have been . . . and diversion from thoughts of darker things, more permanent forms of escape from everything.

At least Lapis was happier, and his treatment of Geren verging on friendly.

A few days after the spill had finally been cleaned up, Lapis came in the door and yelled for him.

Geren set down the skewer of meat he was holding and grabbed a towel, wiping his paws as he trod into the front room.

"You were right!" The wolf looked very smug. "They're all starting to lose big patches of fur. The medicos say it'll only last a few weeks, but they're the ones who told us it wasn't harmful."

"They always say that," Geren said, nearly amused. "I've been through all this before, but at least you took my advice. My shiftmates thought they knew better."

Lapis peered down at him with a look Geren realized contained tiniest mote of respect.

It made him feel slightly pleased, which made him feel slightly ill.

"Well, you're a good boy," Lapis ruffled his hair, then flopped in his chair and lifted his feet for Geren to take off his boots.

Exactly one week later, Lapis slammed in, home early. "You! Get over here."

Geren set the ultrasonic cleaner on the floor and padded over to the wolf, worried.

"We're leaving," Lapis snarled, throwing his bag into the corner. "We're going back to Brynton, this week. Pauli was right, damn her."

Geren gaped. "This week? Brynton? What happened?"

Lapis flopped into his chair, lifting a foot. Geren sprang to, undoing the wolf's bootclasps and trying to avoid the wet red stains.

"Cerion and Albion are drawing down here after the attack. There's civil unrest in other cities. Hasn't spread here yet, but they're offering passes out to us native Brynti, and I'm taking one."

Geren shuddered, stressed. "I can stay in this cottage?"

Lapis stopped and stared at him. His expression was dark, and he looked tense, as though he were ready to spring out of his seat; after a moment his anger seemed to pass. "Yeah, sure . . . I'm gonna let go of the only thing I've got. I'm not in the mood for jokes right now—you're coming with me. No more about that."

"But I'm not Brynti," Geren felt his voice turn up in plaintive entreaty. He raised his paws.

"No, it's alright. As my slave, you'll be listed as baggage. Well, not exactly that, but . . . look, it's ok."

Slave.

Baggage.

He felt like he couldn't get enough air, and he reached a paw out to the wall to prop himself up.

Brynton.

Even the name was proto-nightmare to him. The public image Brynton sold was that of a hard-working tech planet, pumping out industry-leading designs for a fraction of the cost others required. On his home planet of Alaran, however, the persistent rumor was that Brynton's wealth was built on slavery. Nobody quite believed it—Brynton maintained a physical and legal chokehold on information—but Lapis had casually confirmed it, as well as the rumors that Brynton was in charge of Fonaci's industrialization and decline.

If Fonaci was Brynton-lite . . .

He slid down the wall, sinking to a squat. Lapis watched, silent and dangerous.

His engineering school had been clear—avoid all contracts with Brynton, even if the bids looked enticing, and never set foot on the planet.

It was a place from which people never returned.

"Please," he begged, voice soft. "Please don't take me. Please don't take me, please . . ."

Lapis said nothing.

Perhaps, Geren thought, desperate, Lapis didn't know how miserable he was. "I can't . . . I can't deal with it." Words jumbled in his mouth. "I've thought about killing myself. I thought about killing you. I—"

Lapis uncoiled and struck him with a punch to the face—it was so fast that he didn't even have time to flinch. It was the first time anyone had ever struck him in the face, and the first time Lapis had hit him in earnest; the blow sent him, reeling, to the floor, and then Lapis was on top of him, arm raised. The world seemed to waver.

In a daze, Geren stammered a fearful denial, raising his paws to blindly fend off the wolf.

The next blow struck him in the teeth and bounced his head off the wall, and then a knee caught him firmly in the ribs, knocking him flat. Several more punches followed, then he felt the wolf's arms wrap around his head and neck, locking tight, before driving him face-first to the floor once more, all his weight on top.

"You're gonna kill me, tough guy?" The wolf's seething voice was right in his ear, cataclysmically loud, too angry to be mocking. "You gonna kill me, huh?"

"Stop—" Searing pain as lupine teeth closed on a latrinine ear forced his words into a bloody scream, and he choked. Lapis bit hard, then shook, ripping out two of his piercings but slipping free just before he shredded the sensitive cartilage and flesh.

"Gonna kill me? I. don't. think. so."

Geren's vision blurred as the wolf grabbed him by the hair and yanked his head back.

"After all I've done for you, you're gonna kill me?" Lapis' rage grew, uncontained. "You ungrateful little bastard."

Geren blubbered incoherently, trying to explain himself, but found himself entirely unable to form words; he felt the wolf tense for a fraction of a second.

"Wa—"

Lapis drove his head forward, slamming his face into the wall, and consciousness imploded into a haze of shadows, then silence.

SEVENTH

ANGLED RAYS OF THE LATE AFTERNOON SUN, shaved into lines by the window shutters, fell in an orange puddle against the wall of the little cottage's bedroom, lighting the living space in a hazy ochre.

Fenna City was nearing the shortest days of its year, where the sun, on the rare cloudless day, made a tiny loop through the brown haze of the southern sky and then vanished after a few short hours, casting most of the day in dim twilight.

Geren stared at the window, barely aware of anything other than the pain each breath brought, and the knowledge that he'd need to change the slimy gauze pad between his molars soon.

He sat, and breathed, and hurt.

The day after Lapis had beaten him, the wolf had called Pauli had come by to check up on him and repair as much of the damage as she could. To Geren, she had seemed distracted and cold, and her paws were rough . . . but he was in too much pain to protest. After pronouncing him severely concussed, with numerous serious bruises, bone cracks and chips, and multiple missing teeth, she'd said he'd live and immediately took her leave.

Lapis' abuse had resumed as soon as she left.

Geren had refused food that night, and his captor had immediately begun force-feeding him.

When he refused to drink, liquid was poured down his throat.

He was allowed out of his cage, but not allowed to leave the bedroom. He'd forgotten once, and experienced the shock collar activated at full power for the first time; the carpet outside the bedroom still smelled like vomit to his sensitive nose.

Everything was so cold and harsh that it felt like a pre-view of the inescapable life he'd lead as a slave on Brynton, and it seemed worse than death.

Every day brought him one day closer to the date he'd depart for that life. Every painful breath brought him closer to his last breath as a free coyote.

The night prior to the eve of his departure, Lapis had come home drunk, and a particularly bad stretch of reckless, sadistic amory had followed, taking up half of the night. After all the motion stopped and he was put away, he lay in his little cage, bloated from being overfed, bleeding from all manners of injuries, weeping softly in hurt and pain.

All he could think of was how far he'd come in his little life just to end up here.

Looking out through tears and bars, he could see the next twenty years passing by as Lapis' slave. Perhaps he'd be broken by the wolf in a moment of overenthusiasm, or die from breath-play taken a little too long.

Perhaps, once he was worn down enough, he would simply be disposed of, or sold off.

Only ignominious endings awaited to conclude his inconsequential life.

He sighed quietly, imagining himself curled up in Lysi's arms once more. He often sought solace in the thought; despite their fleeting time together, memories of the him always dominated his quiet moments. The handful of hours they'd had, the silly but heartfelt confessions of love, but mostly the passions and emotions, and the desperate, mutual need for affection, that mutual compatibility which had bound them together so instantly and so firmly.

Dazed and broken, he laid his head back and closed his eyes; he missed the fox so very much. He could hear his voice, arguing softly with Coriagh, like some ephemeral whisper on the edge of a dream.

He closed his eyes, trying to focus on what was said; naturally, the more effort he put in, the harder it became to hear, as if his mind acknowledged that the fox was forever out of reach.

A new wave of grief struck him, and he bit his lower lip hard enough to draw blood, stifling sobs lest he wake the sleeping Lapis.

Despite his intent to never bend to the wolf's will, he suspected that he would eventually become his creature whether he intended to or not, even if merely out of habit.

He felt certain that he would eventually lose his grip on Lysi's memory . . . and his sense of self.

The thought sickened him.

For the first time in his existence, he began to reflect on the possibility that life—this life—really wasn't worth living.

Many cultures, he knew, believed that death was just the beginning of new adventures in parallel universes, or resulted in being reincarnated as a new creature. Others held that it was a release to be with those who had gone before, in some utopia where evil had no hold.

From his rationalist upbringing, Geren had always assumed it to be merely the end of an organic process—having seen no magic in his mother's wasting death or his father's simple failure to return home—but the thought that he might have a chance to see his fox again was a comforting, compelling fantasy.

It brought him enough peace that, at length, he was able to find sleep.

The next day dawned cold, and Geren woke to Lapis looming over him. The wolf hauled him roughly from the cage, dragging him into the shower and hosing him down with ice cold water.

Once he'd finished donning his gear, Lapis tromped back into his bedroom to glare meaninglessly at Geren, then slid into his boots and left without another word.

Geren watched him go, then stared down at his paws.

Tomorrow morning, they were scheduled to board a shuttle to the transfer station, and from there a liner to Brynton.

He felt completely dead inside. The morning had brought no surcease from his dark thoughts, and the hurt had only deepened. All he could see was Lysi's face, and all he could think of was his desire to see the fox once more.

Ears perked, he listened for the wolf's runabout to pull away; no sooner had the vehicle receded in the distance than he began searching around the room. He didn't even acknowledge to himself what he was looking for, but in his heart he knew.

Most of the drawers were locked, as usual, but Lapis had left his dirty dishes on the night stand, and one of the utensils was a dull eating dagger.

Geren stared at it, slowly growing cognizant of his intention.

He'd once watched helplessly as a coworker had almost died of an arterial wound from an accident on the lift floor; it had been a horrifying scene, and doubted that he would be able to follow through with inflicting it on himself.

Even the thought broke through his emptiness and evoked a little shudder, and he diverted himself to the cabinet where Lapis stored his grain-derived drinking ethanol.

He'd never liked intoxicants, but he'd heard more than one person refer to ethanol as 'liquid courage,' and that sounded like a useful commodity at present.

He cracked the bladder and tipped it back into his muzzle, suckling it down. It was harsh, but he wasn't drinking for pleasure; he swallowed and swallowed, trying to ignore the taste and the burn in his throat and nose, trying simply to fill his gullet with ethanol.

Once the bladder was empty, he threw it to the otherwise spotless floor, coughing, cringing and belching, mouth and throat afire.

After a few minutes of rummaging around, he flopped against a wall and slid down it to land on his butt, paws balled up around his find—a sheet of waterproof flex-wrap.

Lapis enjoyed controlling his breathing as a method of dominance, so the sensations of hypoxia was not foreign to him. The wolf had taken him right to the edge of consciousness a few times.

He stared at the flex wrap. It seemed both grotesque and somehow pathetic.

All it had to do was work.

"My dear fox," he whispered, eyes moist. "I'm so very sorry it took me so long to find you. Sorry it all ended this way. I'm sorry . . ."

He snapped his jaw shut, trying to hold back useless sobs. The more he thought or said, the longer it took, the harder it would get.

There was no audience to witness a final monologue, anyway.

He took a deep breath, then steeled himself, warm from the alcohol. Firmly, he wrapped the plastic around his head from back to front. After holding his breath for a minute, he exhaled. Reflexively, he drew another breath, and air slid past the plastic with a low-pitched buzz. He couldn't stop himself from taking another, and another.

With a gusty sigh, he tried reorienting it, but had the same problem. No matter what he tried, he simply couldn't seem to get a seal while holding it.

Frustrated and rapidly growing uncoordinated from the ethanol, he tried wrapping it around his muzzle and tying it tightly behind his head; that worked better, but almost as soon as it became difficult to breathe he panicked and yanked it back off, then sat there, queasy, as the room spun around him from a combination of oxygen deprivation and inebriation.

Though he tried twice more, he was unable to suppress his overpowering survival instinct to struggle free. After the last attempt, he flung the sheet away and banged his head hard against the wall, crying out in frustration and disgust, then laid back as tears dripped from his eyes.

He didn't want to die.

He urped and began to hiccup; he could taste alcohol and acid in his mouth. He spat, then wiped his muzzle with the back of a paw, then sat for a while, sick to his stomach, infuriated by how pathetic his suicide attempt had been.

His ears perked at a rustle and scrape from outside, and he jolted upright, a chill sinking into the pit of his stomach.

Lapis simply couldn't be returning yet!

He scrambled to his feet, stomach spasming, then froze in indecision.

If it was Lapis, seconds mattered; if he failed, he'd never get another chance.

Still his legs wouldn't move.

On the verge of breaking down, Geren sank back to his knees, staring at the door . . . but there was no lock beep, no wolf bursting through.

Eventually, determination forced him back to his feet, and he wobbled toward the bathroom. The thought of drowning terrified him almost as much as trying to slash himself open . . . but he knew that if he managed to take a lungful of water that it probably would be over without much more struggle.

Halfway there, he froze—something caught his eye, hanging from the wall of the bedroom.

His leash.

He fingered his collar softly.

The symbolism of hanging himself by it appealed to him, in some strange way.

Gravity, certainly, would never yield to his survival instinct.

He stumbled to the bed and climbed up to pull it down. He knew little about what he was doing, but he knew from fiction and history that it could still work. He was fairly certain he'd need a long drop to make for a quick end; he considered the cage or the bed, but he knew he'd try to climb back up.

He settled on the wolf's foot locker. Standing on end, it was around a meter tall, and he could kick it over.

He retrieved it, looking it over and deciding it adequate. Increasingly confident, increasingly certain, he lofted the metal end of the leash over a ceiling support beam then passed it back through the paw-loop at the other end. He pulled it taut, but found it slightly too long; with fumbling paws, he tied several makeshift take-up knots with increasingly shaky paws until the length was right.

Increasingly fearful, he set the crate beneath the dangling lead, then stepped up onto it, almost as if watching his actions from afar. Turning his collar until its attachment ring was at the back, he straightened and clipped on the double-latch, choking back a little sob of pain, fear and regret.

Tears ran from his eyes to drip from the tip of his nose, and he held Lysi's lovely face in his minds' eye.

"Love you," he whispered.

He swung himself forward to kick the footlocker out from under him, but wobbled; terror shot through him, and he stood back up with a little involuntary curse, coughing and swallowing spasmodically.

After a few moments of calming himself, he settled down into the collar and tried again.

This time, he succeeded in knocking the box over; it skittered well away from him, and he fell forward with an involuntary yelp of fright, which was cut off almost as soon as it emerged.

Under his weight, the leash proved far more elastic than he'd expected, and one of his knots gave partially; instead of the planned quick snap followed by unconsciousness, he found himself choking at the end of the lead, toes banging and scraping on the floor. In breathless agony, he struggled to stand on his tip-toes, clutching desperately over his head until his paws found the leash.

His eyes watered as he struggled for minutes; he couldn't stand enough, and he couldn't pull enough. Eventually, he grew weak, and his body felt heavy and leaden. His mouth hung open, blood dribbling from his bitten tongue; what felt like hours later, his vision at last began to darken around the fringes and grow fuzzy.

Gradually, warmth supplanted pain and he gave in to the pressure from the collar; his sweaty paws slipped from the leash and his arms fell slack to hang leaden to his sides.

As the world grew dark, his mind began to play tricks on him, and he surfed through demi-coherent images of the factory and his recent past, and the bangs and clattering noises of the lifter floor as if he could hear them from far away; to his annoyance, though he bent his thoughts as hard as he could to his foxy love, the last thing he saw before everything ceased was a faint vision of Maven.

Wild dog. The memory bubbled up from nowhere—that's what she was.

Content, he slipped away.

EIGHTH

TEAR-FILLED HONEY-COLORED EYES with wide pupils stared down at Geren from a vulpine face framed with curly, amber hair. He couldn't immediately place them, though they seemed familiar.

He couldn't immediately place himself, either.

"He'll live, I promise. Don't worry so," a friendly male voice with warm, rolled 'r's came from his left. He turned, saw indistinct black fur, then turned back, blinking up at the eyes above him.

They seemed important, somehow.

"Are you . . ." The fox spoke, then trailed off.

Alright?

Alive?

"I don't know." His head hurt. His chest hurt. Many things hurt.

His eyes widened, and he drew in a deep, raspy gasp.

"Lysi!" The words came out in a ragged scream. "Lysi! This . . . but . . . how?"

"Oh my dear yotie," the fox clutched him up into a hug, and he wrapped paws around, squeezing equally tight. Pain shot through every corner of his frame, but he didn't care a bit.

Aeons later, he finally let go, peering up at his lost fox. He started to speak, but his voice was rattly; he cleared his throat and saw crimson spatter the fox's throat.

Confused, he felt around a bit with his tongue—he was missing more teeth, and his mouth was full of saliva and blood.

He sat up, fighting back his pain to take a firm hold of Lysi's paw. "What happened?" His voice sounded strange to his own ears, lispy through his damaged dentition and raspy from a swollen throat. "I don't remember."

"First," The older voice was a little firmer. "I am de-chipping you before you get another casual read. Just say yes."

"Oh. Ok," he said meekly, voice muffled and scratchy to his ears. It tickled, and forced a spate of coughing; when it subsided, he glanced past Lysi's worried face to investigate his surroundings.

He was in a very small, surprisingly clean room. Coriagh and Zori knelt at the foot of his bed, Maven was seated in a chair beside him, and Lysi was leaned over from the opposite side, pleasantly close. Beside Maven was a tall jackal with greying muzzlefur; he wore a blue jumpsuit and synthetic gloves, and goggles sat askew atop his head.

He had a small rectangular box, which he was holding at Geren in a menacing fashion; calmed by Lysi's touch, Geren allowed him to take his paw. The jackal pressed the box directly into the center of his palm, and there was a soft click. A cold sensation immediately spread up his arm, rising from the webbing of his paw, past his elbow, almost to his shoulder, accompanied by the scent of burning flesh.

The doctor—if doctor he was—set the device aside and picked up a small knife, then drew an exact slice directly over the chip.

He swapped again almost immediately to a strange tool that looked like a set of augmented tweezers, and, with an experienced flick of his wrist, popped the datachip free.

Geren stared in mute fascination at the little bio-powered device and its thin strands of filament and wire—that tiny piece of circuitry and encryption, installed beneath one's paw at birth, that marked one as a member of society and allowed one to identify, authenticate, and authorize uniquely.

So easily taken for granted.

Being de-chipped was oddly similar to dying, as far as the system was concerned.

"That simple, eh?" Maven growled over his shoulder, equally captivated.

"That simple." The jackal smiled a friendly smile, then set the chip into a little metal box, which he closed. Two passes of a micro-sized flesh welder later, and Geren was sealed back up with almost no loss of blood. "I assure you that this chip will be completely destroyed. Worry not."

"To answer your question, Geren," Maven broke in, eyes still fixed on the box with the chip, "we found you. I can't believe that we found you when we did, but we found you. Still kicking at the floor. Lysi insisted it had to be . . . but look, after last night, we knew we had to get you today."

"You saw—"

"Why?" Lysi interrupted, voice an emotional whisper. He gave Geren an angry little shake. "Why would you try to kill yourself?"

"I didn't see any other way out," Geren lisped defensively. "I—"

"I would *never* have given up on you," Lysi growled, squeezing his paw painfully hard. "We would have found you. My little hope, for you?"

"He told me you were d–dead, Lysi." Despite the presence of the fox, alive and standing before him, the loss and despair he'd felt the first time rushed back in and almost broke him down. He sucked in a deep breath. "He told me he'd killed you."

"No. Cracked a tooth and knocked me out, but dead? I wouldn't abandon you like that," Lysi rested both paws on his shoulder, his eyes as loving as his voice was gruff. "You stupid thing. Never try that again!"

"I thought I was looking at the rest of my life! And that I didn't have anything to live for outside anyway. I don't know why he came after me, but I was sure he'd never let me go."

"There was this fox, Meryka—Lysi said to us you know her? She found Mally," Maven growled. "Do you want to know what?"

"Well, yes, of course," Geren shook his numb paw, sitting up a little more. Immediately Lysi swung up behind him into the makeshift bed; black paws wrapped around his chest and clung tightly, tugging; he wriggled back against the fox, ignoring the pain.

"She did lots of legwork. Left a frickin' trail of bodies in her wake."

"Mally's my friend," Geren said, worried. "You didn't—"

"Naw, naw. Lysi . . . I don't understand the arrangement, but . . . Lysi reached some kind of agreement with him, and—"

"And," Lysi spoke over Geren's shoulder, "he's fine. I knew him, just by another name."

"So yeah," Maven snorted. "Odd guy. But he did have your back. So here's the deal: I don't know how you seem to attract so much drama for someone so—"

"Mav," Lysi raised his voice.

". . . ok, ok." Maven grinned an acerb little grin, unchastened. "I guess you apparently have some ex—"

"Alain?" Geren was puzzled.

"Is that how you say that? Yeah, him. Anyway, Mally's done quite a bit of digging around since he was fired, and I only wish I knew how. When I think about what I could do with access to . . . well, anyway. I do odd jobs for a guy who knows some people, you know?"

"Get to the point, Mav," Coriagh spoke up; Geren felt Lysi relaxing against him, and frowned as he realized that the fox's paws had become tense.

"Ok, ok, anyway, your ex. The bastard," Maven spat. "He knew you were getting canned. More than knew, actually. It was his idea. Well, his or his mate's, we really don't know. But your group wasn't supposed to be one of the first they got rid of, but they changed the plans."

"What?" Geren sat straight up, staring at her. "I mean, I kinda had guessed he knew . . . but he was gonna destroy my career? My life? And . . . my whole group?"

"Yeah. Well, I don't know. You people are nuts. Like, if I stab somebody or somethin', it's because they were tryin' to stab me." Maven made a little swaying-ducking-jabbing motion. "Or maybe I'm starving, or something, but . . . anyway, not for a long time. And anyway, all these schemes . . . they hurt my head. So yeah, what was it he wrote? I forgot . . ."

"Mally had the company messages," Coriagh filled in. "I don't think she said that part."

"I told her not to," Lysi spoke quietly, though his voice was loud in Geren's ear.

"Oh." The silver fox bit his lip. Geren noticed the tiniest flick of his eyes toward the other two, and felt Lysi make the tiniest motion behind him.

"Alright. The deal's this. Your ex, he wanted you gone months ago, but the termination got delayed, it said,"

"Months ago?" Geren whispered softly, feeling a stab of hurt from an unexpected source; Lysi wrapped tighter, as if trying to keep the pain at bay.

"He wanted you out of the way of his new relation- ship, but didn't want to dump you. I guess he thought you wouldn't take it well? I'm just speculatin' on that last part," Maven growled.

"Out of the way?" Geren shook his head, squinting against his headache, stomach sinking. "It just . . . back then he was still telling me there'd always be a place for me."

"Look, that guy . . ." Maven's expression was fierce. "There was a meeting, and he put you all in. I guess a couple of people got the real deal from him, so wasn't just, like, reading between the lines. Well, anyway . . . he bragged about it a bit, you know."

"I thought I knew him," Geren murmured, staring down. "But I guess I didn't know him at all."

"You not knows until knows," Zori's voice was deep and sad. "Wolf yet are talked about."

Maven bared her teeth. For a diminutive canid, she conveyed an intense menace with shocking ease.

"He—your ex, I mean—paid that Lapis guy off to 'keep you safe.' Real nice guy. Actually, from what we were able to gather, Lapis was *supposed* to make sure you got off the planet, after a few days of play or whatever. So it looks like he reneged on his part of the bargain, too. I mean it—I can't get you people with your schemes and plots, I just—"

"Mav." Lysi's voice was soft and not reproachful.

"I can't believe . . ." Geren lowered his eyes, feeling surprisingly wounded by the knowledge that he'd been so casually and effectively betrayed. "I just . . . I can't believe Alain would do that. I talked to him minutes before they let us go, and he didn't seem any different. And we knew each other so well . . . I thought. I thought he was at least my *friend* . . ."

"Yeah. No. Aaanyway," Maven glared at him, "Mally got worried when you disappeared from the club, and started looking for you. Lapis told him Alain paid him off to get you out, and Mally, well . . . like I said, he was worried about you. He *really* shouldn't have, but he told that wolf about Spencer's club, and from that he tracked you down. We're not quite sure about how, but we think he got close enough to use a chip finder."

"We know how," Lysi spoke, then stroked Geren's chest. "But it doesn't matter now."

"And, hey . . . Mally says sorry, by the way. He also told me to tell you that Hotra and his family made it? All the way."

Geren smiled and nodded to Maven.

Zori cleared his throat, and everyone looked up.

"We is regrets at all time," he rumbled, eyes wide and sincere. "Not . . . not, friend like."

Maven rattled off a question in a strange, musical language, and Zori replied in kind so quickly that it was obviously his native tongue.

"So he says we both feel bad. He means about when we met you, about the whole friends thing, and how we weren't." Maven explained, then waxed angry again. "You know, me, I can't believe what that bastard was doing to you. We got a spydot up, watching for our chance, so we saw all of last night, at the very least."

"Oh." Geren felt himself flush, and he stared down at his paws, picking absently at his bellyfur.

"Sorry for that too, but we couldn't look away. Zori wanted to go in right then, and Lysi was crying. Crying! I never seen him so much as blink before."

"Only because someone else got to do all that to my yotie before I did," Lysi's voice in Geren's ear tried to sound amused and playful, but was too unsteady for either. "But we had to wait for Lapis to leave. He's tough, and armed. And has an alarm box."

"I destroy him if fights," Zori thumped his chest, nostrils flared. He grinned. "But not fights is better."

"We wouldn't have made it out of the compound if we'd fought him, Zori." Coriagh leaned on his shillelagh, shaking his head. "Even Meryka couldn't do it, and she tried . . . remember?"

"What happened?" Geren perked. "Is she ok? There was an effluent spill, and—"

Geren jumped at the tiniest pinch from Lysi, but took the hint.

"Effluent?" Mav looked confused. "I don't know nothing about effluent, but Meryka tried to get in a few nights ago. Said you got beat up pretty bad, but she couldn't do it without setting off some perimeter alarm or something. We didn't think we were gonna make it today, either, but she said it had to be today. She wanted to come, but had something else to do, so it was just us."

"So you came in as I passed out?" Geren wiped his muzzle, and his paw came away bloody.

"I cutted ropes," Zori nodded, passing him a little rag. "Cory holds you up, but, um . . . drops."

"Yeah, sorry about that," Coriagh said, sheepish. "I'm a bit sick and weak. My only contribution to your rescue is your busted face."

"And cutting the collar off, and breaking the door code," Maven said, then snorted. "And getting Doc here."

"I wouldn't have come through the protests for just anyone." The jackal smiled, thumping Coriagh's shoulder. He turned an odd sidelong look to Lysi, then reached out to turn Geren's muzzle up with a paw.

"And his face will heal just fine, minus the teeth I should say. Furthermore, there's no laryngeal fracture, minimal and reducing edema, and no spinal trauma. Oh, he's busted up, but no worse than most people in this city, and he'll be quite fine with just a bit of rest. And he's de-chipped now, so I believe I'm done. Can't do anything for your teeth, though, I'm afraid, mister Geren."

"You have my thanks, Doctor." Lysi murmured.

The doctor nodded sharply. "Of course, Cap. Now, then, I need to destroy that chip and close up here before anyone else comes calling. Nobody's supposed to be in here, and we're ten minutes past the auto-cycle, so it might cause someone to come look."

"We'll go now," Lysi said. "Come, yotie."

Geren shifted out of bed and stood on the floor; his legs wobbled, but Maven supported him. Zori handed him a bundle from his pack; upon investigation, Geren found it to be a new cloak of black fabric, similar to the others'. He slid into it, grateful to be able to hide the signs of his abuse.

It was heavy, but comfortable.

"Thank you, Zori."

"Cory make."

"Just for you," Coriagh smiled softly. "It's what I do. I started on it the night you were taken. Lysi wouldn't let me stop."

"It's lovely, and appreciated." Geren closed his eyes, dipping his muzzle to Coriagh. "But . . . about Lapis? Won't he come just come right back to Lysi's place?"

"We thinks, yes, but leaves," Zori rumbled. "Is agreed."

Lysi nodded. "It's too dangerous here now."

"This part of town? He won't be able find us elsewhere?"

"No. It's . . . it's not him. Things have changed since you were taken. We're leaving the city." Lysi was grim. "It's no longer safe here. Anywhere. I promise I'll tell you all tomorrow. I can't tell you more now."

The jackal paused to stare intently at the fox, and everyone else pricked up their ears.

Only Coriagh seemed unsurprised, Geren noted.

"Cap—" The jackal began, but Lysi shook his head and held up a paw, then tapped the tip of his muzzle twice with a finger in the same gesture the bartender at the Niyoz had made to Geren. The jackal's eyes widened, then narrowed and his stare became surprisingly intense.

"I can't tell anything yet. In case anyone gets captured."

The jackal nodded, then turned and began to stuff his gear into his sack far more hastily than before, joviality melting away entirely.

With a 'come along' gesture to his friends, and no explanation for his odd statements or behavior, Lysi turned and tugged Geren towards the door.

After catching a few hours of sleep in Zori and Maven's little shed to wait out the remainder of the day's light, the five left into the gloom of a deepening dusk, walking past the southern barricades in silence.

A single city guard sat within his armored gate post, head tilted back as he slept.

Though things didn't look different to Geren, the attitude of the little group was far more wary. They moved with stealth, as quickly as their legs could take them quietly, carrying nothing with them save weapons, the clothes on their backs, and a small pack that Coriagh wore containing food and water.

Of them all, only Lysi seemed to know where they were going, and he wouldn't tell anyone.

Through kilometers of long-abandoned suburbs they followed the fox, coming at last to flooded ruins abutting a great river; from the faint light of the city reflecting off the clouds, Geren could see that it was at least a kilometer wide. The black water churned and rumbled malevolently over the broken foundations of the buildings through which it swept, and Lysi paused, spending a full minute deciding which way to go.

Eventually they turned to follow the flood upstream, to the west.

Half an hour later, they came across a steep wall of rocks which bisected their path.

"This is it," Lysi whispered.

"Climb?" Maven's voice was low. "What's at the top?"

"Tube train bridge," Lysi murmured quickly, ears flickering around. "To cross the river. Come on."

The fox started forward, beginning to scale the embankment with his surprising agility. Geren followed, picking his handholds carefully. Every motion hurt, and every stretch was stabbing pain in the ribs, hips, and legs. But the rocks were more even and less steep than they had appeared from the ground, and he forced himself upward until at last he knelt atop the ten meter tall block structure.

Looking back toward the city, he could see the tube extending from both sides in a straight line, its ruined pump-down stations forming supports and leading it into the wall of crumbling buildings that was the near edge of Fenna City, Fonaci's capital. A cold wind rustled his hair, and he pulled the cloak more tightly around him. Looking the other direction, the tube receded into the stygian black, hovering above the deeper black of the roaring, flooding river.

Of them all, only Zori had any difficulty making it to the top.

"No more climbs," he grunted as he flopped down with the rest, shoulders rising and falling as he drew deep, quiet breaths.

"No," Maven chuckled, wrapping her paws around the zebra and kissing his stripy neck. "You're not made for them, are you?"

"This way," Lysi whispered urgently, still standing. "Quiet. Not safe here."

Immediately Zori rose back to a low, supple crouch, and without another word they moved on, heading out on a wide metal catwalk perched atop the tube's girth.

An archaic piece of high-speed inter-city infrastructure from happier times, the tube hadn't seen a train in a hundred years, and it joined its surroundings in slow decay, chipping away to return to the land.

A few meters out over the river, the grating ended; squinting into the gloom, Geren could see wet moss growing atop the perfectly cylindrical structure. He shuddered.

"Not that way," Lysi spoke just loud enough for his voice to carry over the wind and flood. "Here."

A gap in the railing proved to be an access to a corroded ladder that followed the arc of the tube over the side and back down into the dark.

Following Lysi, they descended into the blackness below, alighting on a narrow steel catwalk that stretched between

bridge pylons, clearly intended for inspection or maintenance. Something very cold splashed at Geren's footpaws as
he tried to stay out of the way of those still descending. Blinking into the black, he discovered that they were ominously
close to the floodwater raging under the tube; icy waves
occasionally lapped across or burbled up through the holes
in the thin metal walk, which swayed and creaked alarmingly
with the pressures of the current against its trestle structure.

When at last they had all made it safely down, they set
forward once more. Everyone kept their weight low as they
continued on, clinging tightly to the guardrail.

Geren clutched at the narrow bar of the handrail and
stepped forward carefully, heart pounding; he'd never
been much of a swimmer, and he doubted that even the
best of swimmers would survive the merciless torrent which
frothed and rumbled just inches under his paws. Now and
again, debris would slam into the catwalk, shaking it such
that they were forced to cling to their support and wait for
the motion to subside.

After many minutes had passed, as they passed across
the center of the broad river, Lysi froze, staring forward
intently at something Geren couldn't see.

"Bridges is . . . um . . ." Zori's voice was concerned, looking over the fox's shoulder. ". . . is folding?"

"Bent, Zori." Maven's voice wavered, then turned back
to Coriagh. "The catwalk is damaged ahead."

Coriagh pushed forward to stare along its length.

"Looks like it's detached from the center pylon." He
leaned over the rail, then turned back. "Still connected to
the supports on the tube."

"Do you have any alternate routes?" Lysi spoke quietly,
but Geren could hear the worry in his voice.

"We can't go through this one, and it's probably less safe
atop, with wet moss and nothing to hold onto." Coriagh
sounded troubled. "The closest bridge is a backtrack of

three kilometers, and it's controlled. The nearest uncontrolled crossing is nine and a half kilometers away, and it's probably awash."

"We can go back to my place," Maven suggested hopefully. "Wait out the storm, cross in a few days at a safer point. I can make tea and—"

"No." Lysi spoke firmly and shook his head, an air of desperation creeping into his tone. "We *must* go on. If we can, we must. We can't go back. We don't have time. Hold on tight to the rail no matter what."

As they began to walk forward once more, Geren could at last see what the others were looking at. A long section of the catwalk was heavily damaged, swaying erratically and partially submerged in the turbulent water.

Lysi picked his way forward slowly, as if making sure with each step that there was something solid beneath his feet. Behind him, each followed his lead. Soon Geren's hindpaws were under the surface of the water, which tugged against them with surprising strength.

No sooner had Lysi stepped up to the undamaged section than there was a loud snap; to Geren's horror, he immediately felt himself—and the catwalk—began to swing alarmingly with the current, and a terrible groan-screech filled the air.

He could see little through the black of the night, but in an instant the frigid water was over his knees and he could feel his paws pulled hard by the current.

"GO! GO!" The terrified voice of Coriagh was right in his ear.

"Hurry!" Lysi yelled, voice breaking. "Hold and pull—*Cory!*"

Coriagh lost his footing as the span was submerged, falling into Maven's legs with a yelp; they became tangled, and both were immediately swept over the submerging rail and into the water.

Without a thought, Geren made a desperate lunge, grabbing for the railing and for Maven's belt.

By some miracle, he caught both, holding on for all he was worth just as she lost her own grip on the rail with a little shriek.

The catwalk continued to subduct as it tore away from the tube, pulling him slowly under, but he refused to let go of her or the bar. He struggled to wrap his legs around a stanchion for more support as the water roared across his body, but couldn't reach.

The current was intense, and the catwalk was sinking. The deeper he went, the firmer the pull; as his head and back were submerged, he began to lose what little leverage he had, strength fading quickly. Pain from his injuries rushed through him as rapidly as the water around him, but he held tight, trying to keep his nose above the surface.

He felt Maven's strong, rough paw grab on to his arm to reinforce his hold on her belt, but to his horror he found himself being stretched out like a ragdoll in the turbulent flow.

He could feel his strength failing, and the water was over his head.

An iron vice snapped around his upper arm and began to pull him perpendicular to the current. Within moments, he was able to lift his muzzle free and take gasp of air as he was slowly, carefully pulled from the water. Out of the corner of his eye, he caught a vision of huge, striped muscles standing out like massive cables.

Another set of paws, smaller paws, grabbed his scruff and the fur of his back and began to pull him out with less strength and more desperation. Suddenly the resistance of the load in his other paw went slack, and he clutched desperately at air, terrified that he'd just lost Maven.

Twisting around to look, however, he found that Zori's other arm was wrapped around her waist, pulling her in just as firmly as he was hauling Geren over the rail; moments later, Geren found himself sitting on the wildly swaying span between the zebra and Lysi. He was still clinging to Maven's belt, and Zori hadn't let go of either of them.

Maven clutched Coriagh's empty cloak in her paw and wore a look of shock.

From far downstream, Geren's sensitive ears picked up a faint, desperate gurgle for help, and he tried to get back to his feet, looking futilely around for anything to throw.

"Cory!" Maven called out into the dark, leaned over the rail. She turned back, tugging at Zori's cloak. "We've gotta help—"

"Leave it," Lysi's voice was hoarse but crackled with command. "We must get to land before we lose this catwalk. Move now. Don't run."

Dazed, Geren released Maven's belt and rose to his feet, following Lysi. Zori let go of his arm, and they made their way along just as cautiously as before, even as the walkway began to oscillate in the flow.

The damaged section held just long enough for them to reach the next before, with a soft little scrape and gurgle, it broke away and vanished beneath the surface.

"We must keep moving," Lysi turned back for only a moment. His voice was rough with emotion, wide eyes shining in the wan glow from the city. "Let's hope there are no more damaged sections. Do *not* let go, no matter what."

Geren shuddered, suddenly terrified by the idea that there very well could be a washed-out section in front of them, leaving them stranded mid-stream.

Through the blackness they pressed on.

Many minutes later, Lysi's paw found the ladder on the far side. They all followed him up to the top of the tube and along its embankment.

Lysi looked often down the side, pain in his eyes.

Gradually the path led downhill, and to each side Geren could see only water narrowing its breadth, as if the path was doomed to slip beneath the surface before reaching dry land.

He bit his lip, momentarily frozen in his stride by the memory of the water's icy grip.

To his relief, the high watermark of the black floodwaters eventually gave way to shrubs and trees as worn path returned to ground level.

There they stopped.

"Can we do anything?" Maven's voice was pained, and Zori knelt behind her, wrapping big arms around her chest.

"No." Lysi lowered his head, and Geren could hear the pain in that single word.

"Thanks for saving me . . . again," Geren articulated carefully around his missing teeth, looking up at Zori. The zebra reached forward and squeezed his shoulder gently, eyes sad.

"Thank you," Maven took Geren's paw—hers shook softly in his grasp.

"I'm sorry . . . I want to . . . but we must keep moving." Lysi sighed, running a paw through his hair and closing his eyes. "I'm so sorry, Cory."

Zori made a sad noise, shaking his head. "Good is to not losing alls. You rights to say."

"I agree, if I understand your meaning." Maven sighed. "But I sure hope he makes it."

"He didn't." Lysi raised his head, ears flat, eyes downcast. "He . . . he died."

"But how do you know?" Maven snapped. "I mean, you're gonna give up just like that? He could still . . . couldn't he?" She trailed off into timidity at Lysi's sad gaze and faint headshake.

There was a grim silence, a brief meeting of eyes, and then everyone rose together as if of the same mind.

Geren shook himself softly, shedding a bit of water but mostly trying to clear the chill he felt in his bones.

Hungry, cold, and exhausted, they walked for many hours that long night, following a path worn through the brush. As they got further from the city, conversation began to resume slowly, and they moved with slightly less stealth under the bare-branched deciduous forests, paralleling the old tube train right-of-way for many tens of kilometers.

Lysi led, and not a soul asked where they were going or why as they trod on in silence.

Just as the first hint of a distant dawn began to warm the sky, they came across a narrow, unpaved road. Lysi stopped cold, then whispered for them to stay hidden. The fox stepped forward, sniffing at several trees; after a moment, he turned back and waved them forward, and they followed along the path, carefully staying under the branches.

Not long thereafter, Geren's attention was caught by an orange light shining through the underbrush. He tapped Lysi on the shoulder and pointed; the fox lifted his head, then turned back to Geren with a little nod.

Motioning for stealth, he led them toward the light.

As they closed in, Geren realized that several large shadows in the dark were actually large objects covered in camouflage netting. Further forward, and he could pick out a sprinkle of low-voiced conversation, and smell the now-familiar smell of wood combustion.

More netting was strung over various tents and tables, and the large shapes appeared to be armed, armored caravans, carefully concealed from aerial or thermal reconnaissance.

One lone fire burned low in the center of the encampment, as if to give an obvious reason for the few objects that remained in the open . . . without inviting further scrutiny.

Geren perked his ears, hearing movement in the shadows. Before he could say anything, Lysi straightened and raised his paws.

"Stop."

Two weasels stepped out of concealment, aiming very modern-looking energy rifles at them. They were too far to charge at, and too close to miss. Geren's ears told him that several more guards were concealed in the shadows.

"Identify yourself," the one on Geren's right challenged.

"Captain Lysi of the second, company F. Codeword: Bracer. I'm looking for Meldor Khan," Lysi spoke softly.

Zori and Maven stirred, bracketing the fox with perplexed stares.

The challenging weasel took a half-step forward, dipping his weapon. "The sun rises at dawn?"

Lysi blinked, frowned, then shook his head. "Pass. I haven't checked in for two days."

The weasel's aim returned to Lysi's chest, and Geren felt his heart skip a beat.

"Echoes of Liberty?"

"Shake the fundament."

The weasels looked at each other, then lowered the muzzles of their weapons; a third slipped out of the shadows behind them with a little sensor suite. After a moment of computer-assisted scrutiny, he nodded to the others and they stood aside, each raising a formal salute, which Lysi calmly returned.

Geren allowed himself to breathe, and Zori made an inquisitive noise at the fox, who ignored him with the mildest of shrugs.

"Come," Lysi murmured, stepping through the guards and directing them towards the fire.

Within what turned out to be a surprisingly-effective blind, they came to another table; sitting behind it was another weasel, scarred, wearing an eyepatch and missing an ear. He was studying a large, flexible display showing an area map and cursing softly to himself.

He snapped his head up at their approach, eyes widening as he saw Lysi.

"You! I would have expected to see *you* here." He stood and clasped Lysi's paw, gruff voice almost excited, mouth almost smiling.

"Foxtrot company is with you."

The weasel nodded solemnly, then looked askance at Geren, Zori and Maven.

"My friends," Lysi spoke firmly, lifting his paw to include them all. "Cleared by me."

"Cleared by you, eh?" Meldor arched an eyebrow; he tapped his map, blanking it. "It's good to see you, but how did you find us?"

Lysi stared at Meldor, expression falling to a shade of blank that Geren was beginning to recognize as amused. "Water broke through the partrace. Uncountable dead."

"We know. We knew it would happen with these rains. Is that why you came?"

"You could say that," Lysi rested his paws on his hips. "So what's happening?"

"Well, this city is finally awake, and stirring. Still sluggish, though. Just protests. Ineffective, feeble. We're keeping our muscle out of it. Not so much elsewhere—in Amildar they declared martial law a week ago to quell rioting and suppress risings across the province . . . but their guard is light in number, poorly equipped and poorly trained, and they've killed many civilians."

Lysi shook his head. "That's not what I'm asking. And?"

"And yes, we're slowly trickling reinforcements in to harden their lines. There are many towns now holding out, and lots of villages, especially in the northern regions."

"That's good. And?"

Meldor frowned at Lysi, folding his arms across his chest. "And I have word from Pistar and Jordan Continent, and there are risings there, too. The people are already rioting in five cities, and Jordan governance looks to fall within the week by itself. That surprised me."

"And?" Lysi persisted, teeth glinting behind his lips.

"And . . ." Meldor's eyes narrowed, and he seemed to be considering his words carefully. "What are you asking? Our friends are here."

"So that's it?"

"That's it. Ilion has it now."

Lysi closed his eyes, and Geren could see him shudder slightly by the light of the fire. "Then it's going to happen. I can't believe it took losing the partrace."

"There's not a lot of fire in the hearts of this city, I'm sorry to say. They've done a good job keeping the poor fighting the poor. And without our city, they still have a base of power in the north."

"Yes, yes. So we're moving?" The fox seemed impatient.

Meldor laughed softly. "Don't let my sleepy little group fool you. We'll be packed and moving with half an hour, mark my words. But Ilion's mercenaries have zero hour through thirty. Our job is to exfiltrate our operatives to a staging area nearby . . . but we've got a spot for you and your friends, don't worry. I can't tell you where we're going."

"Meldor . . . I'm captain of foxtrot," Lysi spoke, voice soft. "You do know that, right?"

Meldor sat back, clearly startled. Zori and Maven both looked nervous; Maven's eyes were flicking back and forth, and to Geren it looked as though she actually wanted to bolt.

"My little Lysi? Captain of foxtrot company . . . ?"

"I completed Halcyon myself. I gave the exfiltration order."

"How did that happen? You're the last person I'd expect . . ."

"It's been an odd path." Lysi's voice was soft, ears splayed. "Mostly just necessity. I thought you would know, but we've been running silent for months."

Meldor gazed at Lysi with a meditative expression, and Lysi just stared back blandly.

"What is?" Zori spoke at last, looking baffled. "All this?"

"Revolution," Lysi said, without looking back. He turned his eyes up to the sky. "Rebellion. We're going to take this planet back. Or ..."

Geren felt his pulse quicken anew.

"Or what?" Maven's eyes were wide, ears perked and trembling. "No. I know 'what.' Or we die trying, is that it? This is crazy. What are you doing? How? We have nothing! We can't even stop fighting each other for scraps of food!"

"That's true." Meldor stood, grim. "But *we* are many. All it takes is a catalyst ... and we have friends. Some very powerful friends."

"You can talk in front of them, Meldor," Lysi's voice went raspy, and he cleared his throat. "They're good people. *My* people."

"So you vouch for these ... Captain?"

"I do."

"Very well." Meldor nodded to Lysi, then glanced at his display. His lips peeled back into a snarl; he spat in the dirt, then put his fingers to his lips and blew a shrill whistle. There was a moment of pause, and then the encampment came alive with motion. People spilled out of tents and caravans, and began assembling themselves.

Geren curled against Lysi; there was danger in the air, and much of the conversation eluded him. But he was alive, his fox was alive, and they were together. And that, at least, seemed like enough. It was ever so much more than he'd had before.

He rested a paw on Lysi's shoulder, and the fox leaned slightly into him.

Meldor squinted at him not-quite-dubiously, then turned back to Lysi, leaning forward. "So ... Halcyon. I didn't hear. You completed it? Did you ... ah, deliver the goods?"

"The bombs are in place, if that's what you mean." Lysi said softly, smiling. "I placed many myself. And I will tell my friends everything. They are my coterie. My lieutenants, though they don't know it."

Meldor's eyebrows rose. "Well, then. Captain Lysi. I never would have guessed. Well," his tone changed abruptly, suddenly businesslike and to the point. "Were you able to brief the mercs on the defense network? That's the weakest point in our plan."

"I lost three people on that mission." Lysi's voice was soft, but a shimmer of passion and steel shone through. "But we did. They have an operative named Ash that has been our contact. He has all the data. All we can do now is hope."

"Yes . . . if he succeeds, we win. If he fails . . . well, we might still have a chance."

"The decoys?" Pain shimmered in the fox's eyes.

"Taken by their intel. Our contacts say they've gone for it and committed."

Lysi physically flinched, then closed his eyes for a moment. "Tell me it was worth it?"

"Only if we win."

"Then let's win," Lysi sighed. "So?"

"Let's hope hard." Meldor grimaced. "Otherwise we'll all be picked apart piece by piece after local orbit is cleared."

"Are we falling back to the TRZ? I gave orders to F company to fade to TRZ-A."

"That's still your standing order . . . Captain." Meldor's expression screwed up into a half smile. "We'll get you there."

"Look!" A voice shouted. All activity in the camp paused, all eyes directed up to the sky, where three bright streaks arced gracefully towards the city, reflecting the sunlight high in the atmosphere.

A flash lit the hazy northern sky, then another, then four more in rapid succession.

"Drop shuttles," Meldor said, rolling up his map with increasing alacrity. "Congratulations, Captain. It looks like phase zero is at least partially successful."

"They set off my packages from orbit," Lysi breathed softly, then turned to his group. "Just as planned. The first mercenaries are technicals—they're going to disable the air defenses and command and control. Then a small contingent of shock troops. That's why we left."

"Will the people rise here?" Geren was skeptical.

"I hope so," Meldor interjected. He tossed his map into a bag, then folded up his chair and set it into a small crate. "On that question, among several others, lies this whole venture."

"They will," Maven whispered, then found her voice. "They will. I know my people, and I say they will. Not all of them, but many. Maybe even most. A whole bunch of people just woke up, and they woke up to a world where they don't have to figure out who to kill or shake to get some food. They woke up—"

A distant thump sounded, then a ripple of smaller ones.

There was a thoughtful pause.

"Where are we going after the TRZ?" Lysi broke the silence at last, tilting his head.

"Southward, into the mountains, by different routes. Those of us who survive the automata will rendezvous at a cave system we're set up to use—Ilion's had hundred person crews cleaning and preparing them for months now." Meldor turned, raising a paw. "Hey-UP!"

His yell was answered by a hoot from the other side of the clearing, and Geren looked up as the blind around them was pulled down. To his surprise, the tents were almost all struck and packed, and several caravans were already in motion. Little remained of what had looked like a sleeping encampment moments before but folded grass.

"Is there anything I can help with once we settle in for transport?" Lysi rested his paws on the table and leaned forward, ears splayed.

"No. You're done until you're reformed. For now, anyhow. We'll see what comes up . . . today could be a bloodbath, so keep your command card handy. Number eleven will have room in back for all of you. And yes," Meldor stepped out of the way of young felid who had stepped in to pack his little table, "a few more of our contacts have come in. No suspicion, no mobilization, no response at all as of the 0400 call. Either they're seriously underestimating what they're up against, or they're several steps ahead. We're trying to prepare for both possibilities."

"Of course. And we've done our best, truly."

Meldor smiled. "You deep urban resistance types are so cagey. We just sat back, dropped in orders, and hoped good things happen. Now that I see you here before me, I know my trust wasn't misplaced. At any rate, I must away. If you'll excuse me?"

Lysi nodded.

"Stay alive, people. And trust your fox—he's one of the good ones." Meldor grinned at Geren, raised a paw in an abbreviated farewell to them, then spun on his heel, striding toward his transport.

Lysi straightened and turned back to his friends, eyes deep.

Geren had a million things he wanted to ask; from the looks of things, Maven did too. Forestalling their questions, Lysi raised a little paw, then made a silent 'come along' gesture, ushering them toward a large brown caravan with a small number on the back.

It was conventional in design, long and low on two sets of long, wide tracks, with adaptive camouflage. Its armored back compartment was empty, save a few pallets of gear, and its door hung open invitingly.

As they loaded inside, Lysi took them to the front, against the bulkhead nearest the operator station, then settled himself to the bench with a tiny sigh.

"You're going to explain this, right?" Maven was sharply acid when they'd all settled.

Lysi gazed at the floor, seeming a little shrunk in. "Yes."

Geren moved closer, wrapping an arm around the fox and laying his head on his shoulder; he felt the fox form to him in response, weight shifting slightly against his as his silent support was accepted.

"When I was younger, I wanted to do something . . . to help people. All I met was apathy and defeatism. I gave up. I chose to simply survive. Four years ago, I caught the Denian plague."

Lysi shuddered from nose to tail. "I almost died, like all the rest. Mav . . . when you found me . . . I didn't recover on my own. I was cured. Cured by a doctor from off-planet. An operative. From a race of space-farers called the Dazi . . . He told me I wasn't alone. He recruited me for this."

Geren's ears perked up, and he took a small breath, but held his tongue. He could tell Lysi about Lapis' revelations later. They didn't seem important in the moment.

"Hey!" A hefty, armored badger peered in, silhouetted by the open rear door. "I'm your operator. You guys ready to roll?"

"We are," Lysi spoke up.

"Alright! Ladies and gents, welcome aboard this NT-416 caravan. There are two exits in this caravan—the door in the back, and an emergency hatch top front. Fire extinguisher by each door. There's a fire control panel up front here in case the automated's go out. If you hear two alarm honks, strap in. Four honks, get out and get as far away as you can. Don't check with me, because I'll already be gone. Got it? Good! Enjoy the ride and feel free to buzz me on the intercom."

The badger grinned, tossed a wave, and swung the door shut.

When it had closed, the interior surfaces of the caravan faded away as they began to transfer a projection of the outside in to the occupants.

"Fancy," Maven murmured, but her voice missed acid by a shade, tinged with awe.

"I ran one of a number of cells inside the city." Lysi began speaking again, and all eyes turned back his way. "Reconnaissance. Intelligence gathering. Most of us wanted to flex our muscle peacefully, at first. We're past that now." He shivered. "Several of us, including me, set large bombs at tactically important facilities over the last few days. You know where, Mav."

Maven sat back, eyes wide; she locked eyes with Zori, who looked equally shocked. The caravan swayed from side to side as it began to move, and Lysi raised his head again, eyes narrow.

"We got information about government targets from factory insiders like your Mally," Lysi raised his eyes to Geren, who recoiled in surprise. "And you. It wasn't on purpose, but Meryka was mine."

"I figured," Geren murmured.

"We've been preparing for this for a long time, hoping it wouldn't come to it. Cory . . ." his voice wavered. "Cory was my spotter and confidant. We worked as a team for years."

Zori began to speak, but Maven rested her paw on his chest, holding him back as she leaned forward. "So you're telling me you're with DOCAL?"

"Technically," Lysi smiled a faint, humorless smile, "you are too. Welcome to the resistance."

Maven sat back in stunned silence, resting her paw on her head. "So this is really it. You weren't joking when you said it wasn't safe. If they catch you—"

"We can't allow them to catch any of us," Lysi said. He curled a little more against Geren, who instinctively wrapped his other paw around the fox. "This fight . . . this is everything. It's a desperate gamble. And it's bigger than any of us. Bigger than all of us."

"For me, thinks it good," Zori spoke, reinforcing it with a nod. "Ney ney, times is little."

"Oh, I do too, you know," Maven was a bit gruff. "But all the little shakedowns of government security, all the little thefts from their offices, all the little things I never told this fox about because I didn't want to offend his sensibilities . . ."

Lysi smiled. "I knew about them, Mav. Kruuk was one of mine."

"He—*yours*? And he never said . . . wait, wait. Was?"

"He died a few weeks back." The fox's smile fell slightly, tinged with sadness. "Caught within the perimeter and beaten to death by factory security."

Zori pounded a fist impotently into the bench, and Maven clenched her jaw, trembling with an unidentifiable emotion.

"Cory and Kruuk? And violent revolution, mercenaries in the city, and we're *bombing* things, and you never told us *anything*? And we're just rescuing your coyote like nothing's happening?" Maven frothed.

"It's going to get much worse. Much worse, Mav. May not be much better within our lifespan," Lysi said. He clutched his paws together, leaning forward over his knees and looking down at his hindpaws. "Our normal lifespans, anyway. No telling how long we'll survive. Death has been our constant companion . . . we simply must become better-acquainted."

"Can't like it live," Zori said, resting a paw on Maven's shoulder. "Like it . . . was it."

"What does that even mean? All these years and you're no better at standard?" the round-eared canid snapped, spinning to glare at Zori, who looked hurt.

"Easy, Mav." Lysi murmured.

"I means," Zori still looked hurt. "Lives if we . . . as we was, cannot."

Maven sighed, closing her eyes and hanging her head. "We can't live like we've been?"

Zori nodded, expressive eyes wide. "Makes apologies, at standard."

"No, no, none needed," Maven shook her head. "Just, you know . . . It felt like . . . no matter how bad it was getting in some ways, life was getting better for us, and stabler, and . . . you know. We had our farm, and our little band . . . And to see . . . To lose Cory like that . . . He made the belt that Geren held onto me with. It didn't fail me . . . but I couldn't hold him. I . . . and now Kruuk? I didn't hear from him, but I never would have thought . . ."

Tears welled up in her eyes, and Zori wrapped big arms around her, squeezing tight. Lysi withdrew a bit, silent for a few minutes.

"This wasn't how I wanted it," the fox murmured, then trailed off. When nobody spoke, he lifted his head, eyes glowing in the wan light of the caravan. "It wasn't. But it's . . . it's how it is. I will go with it. I've seen so many deaths . . . so many deaths. Even if it all ends, it will be better."

Mav was breathing deeply, and Zori looked sick.

"But," Geren almost surprised himself by speaking, "those at the factory, those with means, those with resources . . . I don't know how the government here works, I'm . . . embarrassed to admit, but . . . *can* this hurt anyone but the poor?"

"Yes." A very slightly predatory smile touched the fox's lips, and for the first time Geren caught the veiled hint of steel behind his eyes, deeper and darker than he'd realized the fox was capable of. "The government . . . they learned from Brynton. But they didn't want to spend the money Brynton did. Learned to set the poor against one another to effect control. They have nothing to counter this."

They sat in silence. Geren traced random patterns into Lysi's backfur, paw tucked beneath his cloak.

"I wish Cory had made it," Maven said, then closed her eyes and hung her head. "The bastard had all the food."

Nobody said anything; everyone could see the tears dripping from her nose. Geren fingered the cloth of his cloak and shook his head, swallowing his own emotions and turning to watch the world go by outside. The trees darkened as the caravan went on, and the terrain began to undulate beneath its frame as they slid deeper into the forest on the little mono-track.

For many hours, there was little conversation. Zori curled up into a surprisingly small curl at the forward bulkhead, and Maven stretched out on the bench beside him, and slept. Though in constant contact, Lysi seemed withdrawn, and eventually Geren laid his head on the fox's shoulder and closed his eyes.

"My world," the fox said, startling him awake some time later, as the darkness was growing once more in the hints of sky visible through the trees. "My whole world has always been small. Do you wonder why I came up to you at first? Danced with you?"

Geren bit his lip. He'd been afraid a conversation like this would be forthcoming.

"If it wasn't my rakish good looks and coyote charm . . ."

"No," Lysi seemed intent on being serious, holding eye contact with him. "I have a . . . thing . . . for outsiders. For . . . for contaminating something pure."

Geren took a deep breath, summoning all the self-control he could muster. "So you've done that before, then?"

"Yes, often. Does that bother you?"

"If it does, the fault doesn't lie with you," Geren suppressed a sick feeling, grinning a wan little grin. "I'm sorry if I came on too strong, but—"

"—So you actually meant it when you said you loved me, you silly thing?"

Geren swallowed again, trembling. "I . . . yes, I—"

"—And you believed me when I said I loved you?"

He hung his head. "Yes," he whispered.

"Good," Lysi's paw found his chin and held it up, forcing eye contact. "Good, because I do. I love you for your vulnerability. I love you for your touch, and your innocence. Those from the factory who slum with locals mostly do so to fulfill fantasies they can't get inside."

"I—"

"I love you, and I won't let you forget that ever. I choose to love you, Geren. I liked you when you danced with me. I stopped thinking of you as a target then. I loved you when you abandoned everything. When you climbed the wall. Climbed, despite your fear. I . . . You are my yotie, and I am proud of you. I am warmer when you're near." Lysi's voice was earnest, but passion lent his words weight and pace and Geren was hypnotized. "If you hadn't been taken away, I . . . I might have abandoned the resistance and convinced you to come make a life with me out of the city, away from the fighting. If you had died," he paused, eyes moist for the first time Geren had seen, "I would have ignored my orders. I couldn't have taken it. I don't know what I would have done if I hadn't met you. It can't un-happen."

Geren reached his other paw up to stroke Lysi's cheek. The fox closed his eyes and rubbed his cheek against his pawpad, then gently grasped his paw in his own.

"But I may have committed us both to death," Lysi's soft voice held a frisson of worry. He opened his eyes and turned them up to Geren, letting a little more emotion through. "I already led Cory to his."

"You don't think . . ."

"No. He's dead," Lysi's voice was solemn. He lifted a little silver dot from a pocket and held it out to Geren, then dropped it back in.

"What is that?" Geren asked, tilting his head.

"We have—we had—mutual monitors. Mine went off when he died, and I took it off."

"What are they for?"

"They're so if either of us died the other would know to get out."

Geren hung his head. The caravan wiggled side-to-side as it passed over a small log, and Lysi used the motion to rise silently to his feet, tugging Geren to his and then toward the back of the caravan, several meters away from his sleeping friends.

"I don't want to do this, yotie," Lysi's voice trembled softly as he sank down on the bench. "I don't want to fight for this. I've tried for most of my life to change this place with peace, but now I've killed friends I love and enemies I don't even know. I just want to escape and be with you."

"Yours is a good cause. There's a saying I once heard," Geren said slowly. He tilted his head, trying to remember exactly. "'We don't choose our lives, but sometimes our lives choose us.'"

"But I chose you," Lysi said, sounding almost frustrated. "What more can I give to a rebellion? Millions may die. Win, all is destroyed and we start over from nothing. Lose and we're infamous. Terrorists. Hunted for the rest of our lives, and they'll be short lives. At least . . . before . . . it was stable before."

"Dear fox." Geren clutched Lysi's paws in his, his sibilants hissing through his broken teeth as he spoke. "I've been on four worlds. Never seen or heard of one like this, except Brynton. I had no idea, when I was inside—No," he interrupted himself as his thoughts collided. "No, that's just self-deception. None of us inside wanted to think about what was outside. Horrible, yes, but we blamed you. I don't want to practice that sort of self-deception anymore. Every day I've been with you has been real, every moment visceral and pure, and you've given me hope . . . but look around you. If the rest of the planet is anywhere near as bad as that city, what do we live for? Stability? Lapis was stable, but I tried to kill myself to get away, and I'm no theist. If you fight, I will fight. I'm not much of a fighter—he showed me that—but surely this won't be a battle of strength."

"No," Lysi sighed, tugging Geren against him. "But for the first time in my life, I have something to live for."

Geren folded into Lysi's arms and wrapped his paws around the fox. His swollen throat was sore from talking.

"Then let us try," he whispered softly, directly into the vulpine's black ear, "to stay alive."

"Until this is all over." Lysi clutched him tightly.

"Until this is over."

Sheets of frigid mist rolled and twisted from dark umber skies, swept by icy gusts across a broken urban landscape lit mostly by firelight and the few sections of city where power remained. A bone-deep chill soaked countless thousands of emaciated forms, biting through fur and fabric alike. Above the streets and courtyards loomed the foundations of silent towers and megastructures, rising ominously into the low overcast. Few lights shone from their glistening silhouettes, and once-bright signs and displays were now blank and silent.

One stocky structure, of a different design and in better repair, stood alone in an orange wash of light; razor wire and a large concrete wall seemed to hold back the labyrinth of dark buildings surrounding it.

The guard posts were empty, one section of floods was dark, and part of the wall lay smoldering in the courtyard, concertina wire dangling obscenely into the gap.

Inside the perimeter, in an improvised alcove barely sheltered from the drizzle, four armored forms sat in a tense hush, broken only by the soft whistle of the icy wind. The smell of spent explosive and ozone hung in the air.

One figure, much smaller than the rest, hunched over a terminal display, fur and accessories illuminated by the soft red glow. He lifted his black-furred paw to wipe the moisture from his helmet visor, pupils wide in his anxious brown eyes, then tucked closer to the dimly-lit surface as a chunk of concrete and masonry fell to the flagstones outside.

"Five minutes, Adran." A gruff, worried female voice over his shoulder echoed the red countdown projected on the inside of his visor. "Doable?"

"I think so," the armored fox whispered, almost to himself.

The seconds were flying by.

He wrenched his attention away from the chronometer, wiping his paws on his thighs to conceal their anxious trembling.

"Frag it. Come on. There's no way, Neyla." Another voice chimed in, higher-pitched, grating on Adran's taut nerves. "We're outta time. I—"

The sharp single crack of a projectile weapon reverberated through the darkened buildings outside. Seconds later, a muffled crump of suppressing fire resonated through the pre-dawn fog, and silence returned.

Adran shifted his weight to steal a glance down between his legs at his little homemade exploit module. Its small display cast a soft green glow on the tangle of tap wires running through the hastily-cut open network conduit.

Thirty two. Fifty four. Ninety six. Every detected frame brought him closer to success, but every second that passed on the mission timer brought them all closer to death.

He let his breath out through his teeth. If he'd inserted the vampire taps on the right busses, if they hadn't triggered an exception, if the alarms were suppressed, if the stolen keys were real . . .

. . . An excerpt from *Ephemeris*
Book Three in the Draconyma Cycle

ABOUT THE AUTHOR

Sasha Fox is an airline pilot and author from the wilds of San José, California, where she lives with her dearest kitty and writes away the hours she finds herself free.

When not plying the skies or writing, she can be found playing hockey, fighting with swords, or camping out under the stars in her beloved Alaska.

http://foxprints.org/